Jennifer Hayashi Danns, author of The Mu Chronicles, is a Scouse writer who spent a decade in Fukuoka, Japan teaching English, raising her very genki children and finding time to explore active volcanoes and iridescent caves. She is an alumna of Faber Academy online and has published short stories and poems in various anthologies.

Jennifer loves Siamese cats, pistachio ice cream and David Bowie's goblin king in *Labyrinth*.

jenniferhayashidanns.com

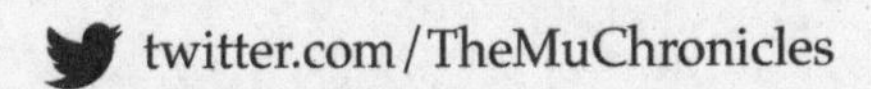

Jennifer [illegible] Lane, author of [illegible] [illegible], is

a [illegible] who spent [illegible] [illegible] in [illegible] [illegible],

teaching English, raising her seven children and

finding time to [illegible] [illegible] [illegible] [illegible]

[illegible] [illegible] [illegible] Academy [illegible] and

has published short stories and poems in various

anthologies.

[illegible] [illegible] [illegible] pistachio [illegible] and

[illegible] [illegible] [illegible] [illegible]

[illegible]

[illegible]

ACROSS THE SCORCHED SEA

The Mu Chronicles: Book Two

JENNIFER HAYASHI DANNS

One More Chapter
a division of HarperCollins*Publishers*
1 London Bridge Street
London SE1 9GF

www.harpercollins.co.uk

HarperCollins*Publishers*
Macken House, 39/40 Mayor Street Upper,
Dublin 1, D01 C9W8, Ireland

This paperback edition 2023
1
First published in Great Britain
by HarperCollins*Publishers* 2023

Jennifer Hayashi Danns asserts the moral right to
be identified as the author of this work
A catalogue record of this book is available from the British Library

ISBN: 978-0-00-849121-5

Printed and bound in the UK using 100% Renewable Electricity
by CPI Group (UK) Ltd

For Bethan Morgan.

And rebellions of love.

Author's Note

Across the Scorched Sea continues to explore the origin of gender and the story uses neopronouns.

Pronouns can be used to identify a person instead of using their name. He/him/his are masculine pronouns. She/her/her are feminine pronouns. Many people also now use the singular "they".

On the now submerged ancient island of Mu, the Maymuan people used mu/mem/mir.

New (neo) pronouns can be used instead of traditionally gendered pronouns or the singular "they".

For example:

She waved at her friend.

They waved at their friend.

Mu waved at mir friend.

I invite you to sail with me across the scorched sea where we will find out what fate awaits forbidden twins Kaori [KAA–ow–Ri] and Kairi [KAA–i–Ri].

I hope you will embrace all you find there.

Content Notice

Dear Reader,

Across the Scorched Sea explores various themes, including violence. I hope this book can be a place to safely explore difficult topics.

The fictional characters commit acts of violence against themselves, each other, and animals. There are graphic scenes of ancient sacrifice rituals. There are scenes of extreme mental distress, self-harm, and suicide.

The devastating consequences of violence are also explored in this book. I hope we can deeply reflect on the futility of violence then reject it in all its forms and choose love.

If at any time you feel overwhelmed, please take a step back, and if you want to discuss your feelings about violence, mental distress, self-harm or suicide I strongly urge you to use the resources listed below.

Love,

Jennifer

Childline (UK)

0800 1111

www.childline.org.uk

Support for children and young people in the UK, including a free helpline and one-to-one online chats with counsellors.

Samaritans (UK)

Call 116 123 (freephone)

Email jo@samaritans.org

Write a letter to Freepost SAMARITANS LETTER

Online resources at www.samaritans.org including free Samaritans self-help app

Samaritans are open 24/7 for anyone who needs to talk.

Scroll Three

ONE

Takafumi

Blackland - Orbit Two

Shadows prowl in the flicker of Takafumi's torch. Flashes of a banished red robe peek from beneath his dark cloak as he strides to the destiny denied him by cockroach Kaori.

Takafumi smiles thinking of her, prone, in her gilded chamber beside Ren, a restless reminder of her twin. He looks so much like Kairi; she probably sees herself in those blazing brown eyes but those who long for the island see Kairi.

He will return. He would never leave them there in Blackland. With her.

Blackland. Named after the lush soil nurtured by Kaori's Nile. Takafumi creeps across Redland, the expanse of desert beyond the settlements of Blackland, sparse and devoid of water; a place for traitors to tread.

Takafumi searches for footsteps swept away by the tides of the desert. He squints into the night for any sign of others disturbing the sand. Wind swirls warm air across the vast open plain, whipping up sand to bend and contort in futile flight from the stifling heat. Grains crumble beneath his feet, guiding him down a gentle slope towards a gaping black hole. His flame illuminates a low, dark mouth with a craggy upper lip. Murmurs bubble and froth within. Takafumi enters.

Fangs protrude from the ceiling of the cave. Pockets of fire burn in the cavities on the floor. More teeth protrude from the sand, ready to snatch those too willing to forget Mu.

"Namu Kai," Takafumi says.

"Namu Kai!" roar the mottled-armed crowd, panting with pleasure at the arrival of their leader. They brandish a dark iridescent feather. The symbol of the Kai.

Takafumi peels off his cloak and a thrill ripples through them. They eat the red robe and chew the soft fabric, savouring all that she has denied. Other Experienced join Takafumi, though not all. They aren't reckless; they will never replace her without patience. They also shed their skin and any pretence of civility is abandoned. The frenzied crowd tear strips, licking and sucking each piece, moaning, eyes squeezed shut, tongues licking the fanged roof in ecstasy. Saliva begins to drip from the ceiling fangs and the fire pits sizzle.

Experienced Takako and Taketo exchange a glance and nod at Takafumi. It is time.

Takafumi wipes sweat from his forehead, overwhelmed not only by the heat of the pit and the fever of the mob but by the knowledge of what is to come. Takako approaches the altar that has been eagerly clawed into the sand. The opposite of a grave, it is an elevated mound surrounded by a deep trench. Takafumi watches her enter the trench. She looks strange without her dreadlocks resting on her hips, as do he and Taketo without their silver nests perched on their heads. She hacked them off, replacing them with a short helmet of braids dyed black with the ink of crushed nettles. No grey in her Blackland; no respect for those who have lived longest. No honour. Only her and her followers adorned with gold. Takafumi had remembered to remove his gold before entering this fray. And the new glyphs from his mouth.

Not only he and she but son and daughter. Boy and girl. Man and woman. In Kaori's land, they are opposite but equal. No longer Maymuans. All are united and referred to by the glyph "people"; those with fewer than twelve orbits referred to as "children". With so many stolen pods full of Kairi's acolytes, Kaori had no choice but to honour the split. Takafumi despised her attempts to appease those loyal to Kairi and was quick to remind others of Kairi's original intent. May and mu. He and she. May rules mu. He rules she.

Memories as sour as forgotten ganba cannot delay the ceremony any longer. Takafumi lies on the altar. Determined his trembling hand will not betray him, he whips open his robe and removes his creased arm from his sleeve. The altar shifts and crumbles a little. Takako gently raises Takafumi's wrist above his head, exposing the soft underarm flesh. Fire blazes as the mob crowd the banks of the trench, shadows scuttling to peer from the ceiling. Water sloshes as life writhes in a sealed woven bag. The crowd part to allow Taketo entry.

"Children of Kairi!" Takako bellows.

"Kai!" they shout.

"The Kai!" Takako continues.

"Kai!" they reply.

Takafumi's exposed chest heaves. Sweat trickles down his wrinkled skin.

"Here in the Redland, we gather where water cannot penetrate. Where she cannot flow."

"Kai!" they shout.

The prickly spines of the ceiling glisten, an angry sharp droplet formed long ago sneers at Takafumi. He closes his eyes.

"We honour him, we see him, we are *he*. Takafumi, lead us to He. Lead us to He!" Takako screams.

"Kai," Takafumi murmurs, teeth bared and clenched.

Silence falls. Even the branches feeding the pits refuse to crackle.

Taketo draws the jellyfish from the bag, not quite the blue of the ones on Mu but as eager to maim.

The cave fills with Takafumi's screams.

The Kai scatter, careful to return to the Blackland before dawn. They will tell the others how Takafumi writhed and rolled into the trench. How they saved him, laid him on the altar, and held their spit-soaked palms on his wound until it no longer burned.

There is no more doubt.

The end of she has begun.

TWO

Kaori

Blackland – Orbit Four

Beneath the water, I can breathe. It is cool and calm until silver bees swarm my eyelids, forcing me up for air. The sunlight stings my eyes and the noise… Always noise. There are too many people here. Always here. Bare feet slapping the tiles, fingernails scratching endless plates of fruit, necks creaking in eternal bows.

"Why are there so many of them?" I ask.

Saki laughs and flicks the Nile water, which flows beside the temple, at me. "Does someone need some honey?"

And of course Eri rushes over with my robe, a plate of honeycomb, and a deep bow of respect. I reach for my robe. "Thanks, Eri."

She blushes.

"Where is Ren?" I ask.

Eri smooths a stray hair from her forehead with that horrible mottled hand – a grim souvenir from her time on Kairi's side of Mu. "He is studying glyphs in his chamber."

I smile. "You mean tearing up pieces of scroll and pleading for extra figs?"

"Yes," Eri says, finally meeting my gaze.

Ren loves her. Other than Saki, she is the only one who can make him laugh until he snorts like a boar. But she never speaks beyond answering my questions. I know why Ren likes her, she has a lovely open face and the same energy as him – the spark of those who have not seen too many orbits. On Mu she would soon leave the Experienced, at the end of her twelth orbit, and be given an island duty, but here in Blackland she serves us in the temple.

There are not enough people from my pod to serve in the temple. I must lead by example and allowed those scarred by Kairi into my personal chamber. Well, that is what I tell myself. My heart does not always agree. Neither does Saki.

I rise from the water and Eri turns away from my naked shell while holding out my robe. I wrap the soft white fabric tight and follow Eri up the stone steps into my private chamber. Saki enters sucking honeycomb and closes the door behind her. The golden honey drips down

Saki's arm. Eri leaves to prepare my jewellery and robes and I pull Saki on to my lap and suck the honey from her fingers.

Eri returns and Saki leaves us to dress. I have to satisfy my hunger by biting the honeycomb where Saki's mouth has been. I gave Blackland doors yet I never have privacy. There is always someone waiting to attend to my every need. Except my need for privacy.

I sit down on my chair and watch Eri pound the seeds to oil my hair. Is her life better here than it would have been on Mu? I mean, of course I am not forcing her to mate for Blackland then hoarding all her children in my pyramid but, I don't know, sometimes I wonder what Mu could have been if I had only controlled the tsunami and let Kairi go.

Ouch!

"Sorry," Eri whispers, leaping back from combing my hair.

I reach up and wrench my long-toothed hair pick from a tangled knot in my hair, "Mymig it!" I shout and Eri cowers even further back.

"I am not shouting at you," I shout, "but hurry up and get rid of it."

Eri scurries to light a candle and makes to cut the knot with the flame as she usually does with the ends.

"For ratty hell's sake, that is not going to do it, is it?"

She just stands there holding the lit candle. "Here, use this."

I rise and pick up my long dagger from the table beside my bed. Eri looks as if I am trying to hand her one of the black Nile snakes, not my gorgeous dagger. It is the shape of an ankh. The handle is mother of pearl and the blade waits in a snake skin sheath.

"Here, take it." I make her grab the handle.

I sit back down and wait for her to chop off the clump of hair. The blade flashes in my large round metal mirror and a shock of jellyfish shivers my spine. I turn to face the girl and see her staring at the sharp tip. I lunge at the dagger and she backs away and trips onto the floor.

"Give it to me!" I hiss and snatch the dagger from her hand.

Eri is wide-eyed with fear and fat tears begin to fall. The door opens and Saki returns. Eri flees.

"What is going on?" Saki exclaims.

"Look!" I cry. "Look what she did." I drop my robe and show Saki my back.

"There is nothing there," Saki says.

"What do you mean there is nothing there? She stabbed me!" I touch the top knot of my spine where the blade pierced.

"Kaori. There is nothing there."

I search my hands for blood but there is none. Just a

terrified child I bullied to the floor. *Bahm*. What is wrong with me? I slump into the chair.

Saki frowns with concern. "I'm sorry, Kaori, but something has happened."

She glances nervously over her shoulder at the door. "You will have to resolve it. There has been another fight outside the temple."

Oh for ratty, *ratty* hell's sake. What is wrong with these people?

"You need to hurry, so can I send Eri back in?"

I nod.

Eri returns and manages to avoid looking at me even more than usual.

"I'm sorry," I say.

Eri nods.

I touch her shoulder but she flinches. *Forget it then, you ungrateful little mouse!* I grab my dagger and slice off the matted clump of hair. It lies between us as Eri begins to weave my remaining hair into braids, oils my skin, and dresses me as though I am as swaddled as Ren.

My gold bangles rattle and echo in the lofty main chamber of my pyramid. Before me kneel two wretched Blacklanders. One is staring with such hatred I am almost impressed. The other, in many ways, is more terrifying because he is staring with such pitiful devotion that my stomach churns. They are both dressed in the plain brown robes of those who do not serve in the temple. But only one has an arm covered in angry scar tissue. The chamber is lined with various decorated temple leaders, unfortunately including Takafumi and the other former Experienced. Takafumi is watching how I deal with this situation with his usual smirk.

"What happened?" I ask, though I already know. There is a different pair with the same story nearly every rise.

The scarred one snarls and the other rushes to explain.

"This … this *beast* … attacked me! I was selling my bread from my stall and he struck me. Look!" he says, pointing at a small bruise blooming above his eyebrow.

The scarred shakes his head.

"You did!" the baker continues. "I can bring others here; they will tell you the same!"

"What. Happened?" I ask again, banging my long staff against the stone floor. My cold tone snuffs out the hysteric.

The scarred fixes me with an unblinking stare. "I made that, you know."

What the ratty hell is he on about? The leaders rustle. Takafumi's eyebrow lifts.

"That?" he sneers, pointing at my gold snake head

staff. "What? Did you think it came out of the mine like that?"

My palm sweats over the staff's gaping hood. Saki shuffles in discomfort beside my throne.

He continues, "But I can't eat it, can I?"

"Well, you can't poison it either," snaps the baker, finding his voice again.

"So am I correct in saying this is about you wanting a new duty?" I ask the smith.

He laughs, a horrible high-pitched sound that curdles my tongue. "No. I want much more than that."

This is worse than the other squabbles I have seen. Much worse. Clouds block the light from the sun entering the slits of the upper walls. In the flash of dark, the smith stands.

"Namu Kairi," he begins to chant and numerous guards who also share the scars on his arm drag him from the main chamber. The space erupts with the assembled unmaimed protesting their indignation.

"What will you do with him?" Takafumi drawls, and only the sound of my staff scraping the tiled floor can be heard.

I have absolutely no ratty idea.

"He will be dealt with," I say.

"Of course he will," the baker simpers, getting off his knees. "You are our one and only leader."

"I know what you did," I hiss.

"Kaori," Saki warns.

"Who? Me?" the baker stutters. "Look, look what he did to my face!"

"You spat at him. As he passed your stall," I say.

The baker's jaw slackens. "I would never."

I swing my staff and nudge him back onto the floor. I stand and thrust the gold snake face in his. "Next time this will be black and from the Nile."

He stumbles to his feet and scurries out into the courtyard.

Saki is pacing around my chamber and I am fighting the urge to impale her with my dagger.

"Why are you so determined to disturb every single person on Blackland? He was on your side! What do you think is going to happen when they realise that their loyalty means nothing to you."

I can't stand this anymore. I stop fumbling with the snake sheath and throw my dagger over Saki's shoulder. She ducks and screams.

"Take these as well." I pull my ridiculous bangles from my wrists and throw them at the wall. They clang and rattle on the floor. "Why do I have to wear these ratty things? Who made these? Kentaro?" Saki flinches at the mention of his name. "Or was it Ikki? Or Aito?" I sob.

Saki shakes my shoulders. "You have to stop this," she says. It is a command not a plea. "For me. And for Ren. We won't survive this if you continue."

I can't hear her. I have to go.

"Where are you going?" Saki says.

"I can't be here. I need to … go. Anywhere," I say and head for the door.

Saki grabs my wrist and drags me to my mirror. "Look at yourself, for ratty hell's sake."

I see my twin, afraid of what is stirring within and bursting out.

"You can't be seen like this." Saki pushes me into my chair and washes my face with a wet piece of fabric. "Eri? Eri?" she calls.

Eri unfolds herself from the corner of my chamber. She tucks herself so far into my shadow I forget she is there.

"Please fix Kaori's eyes and repaint her arm glyphs," Saki says and reaches to pick up my tossed jewellery.

Eri's hand trembles as she dips the brush into the ground galena, but she manages to ring my eyes in black and my mask is restored.

Saki and I pace the grounds of the temple.

"Can't we walk around the stalls outside? You keep

saying I have to please these people. Wouldn't they be happy to see me out there?"

Saki gives me a withering look. "No."

I don't know how much longer I can endure this. It seems like a life cycle ago when I could lie in the cove, or even sail the slimy river to the waterfall. Now I see the same view every rise. My chamber, Ren's chamber, the main chamber, the courtyard, these ratty gardens.

"Why not?" I ask.

Saki points to a Blacklander tending the jasmine in a large urn by the central pond. The sweet, heady scent reminds me of hunmir. I shiver.

"What?" I say.

"Look at her chest," Saki whispers.

With each snip of her shears the gardener's robe gapes. Her skin is covered in scar tissue.

I clutch Saki's arm. She nods. "We have to be careful, Kaori. I have seen a few of them now who have gone full Kairi – legs and feet covered in welts and scars."

Kairi. My twin. We were two halves who never slotted together; easily torn apart by zealous Takanori until we literally lived on opposite sides of the island of Mu, divided by a volcano of Kairi's creation. The price of entry to Kairi's side was an arm lashed by a jellyfish. Even now, after we sailed in opposite directions for countless orbits, he is here. In the skin of this woman who has the audacity to tend *my* garden outside *my* temple with arms and legs freshly maimed declaring her allegiance to my twin.

The gardener notices us and bows deeply then leaves the garden. Saki and I sit on the lip of the pond. A blue lotus bud bobs. I dip my finger in the still water and it begins to churn. The lotus sails to my palm.

"It is time to flood the Nile," I say. Ever since I struck the skies and a blue snake – the Nile – coursed through our new land, we have been rich in black soil and lush vegetation on its banks. The land beyond, however, is still extremely dry, so once an orbit I must flood the banks and soak our settlement with Nile water. The blue lotus tells me when the blue snake must rise again.

Saki looks at the lotus. "Maybe in two more rises?"

Yes, then the lotus will bloom and open for only three rises. At dawn, curious blue petals unfurl, taste sunlight, and wilt. Glad to be alive; born in water; at ease in the muddy pond.

"We could do with some blue wine," Saki says, a smile playing on her full mouth, "You certainly could."

I laugh. It feels good.

"You should be proud," Saki says. "Look at all you have built."

"*We* have built," I say.

The temple rests beside the Nile. It took six moons for Blacklanders, scarred and unscarred, to dig the trenches for the boats to rest full of stone. Takafumi as usual tried to take over and build as they did on Mu, hauling stone piece by piece over land, each Maymuan soul extinguished during the process considered a worthy sacrifice. I knew we only needed a pack to load the stones from the quarry and a pack to unload and build. I would carry the load. And so it was. I sailed my pyramid down the Nile without one Blacklander life lost.

We need to build and unite again.

"We have to make the Nile ceremony this orbit as mixed as possible," I say.

Saki sighs. "We can try but I'm not sure, Kaori. What the baker was saying about them poisoning the bread is… I don't know. We have to be careful."

"Them? This is what I mean, Saki; there is no them! There is only us, all stuck here together. If they want to poison everyone then I should have left them bobbing in the ratty pods."

Saki looks at the jasmine abandoned by the gardener. "What do you want to do?"

"Make sure that it is not only the temple Blacklanders on the banks of the Nile." I should give them the Experienced spaces. I could do without their glares. "It is always white robes – make sure there are some brown robes too. Why have they all ended up being guards or gardeners anyway?"

Saki gives me a long look. "People like order. They

like to have someone above and they need someone below."

"Well, that is ridiculous," I say.

"Is it?" Saki says. "You could resolve all this conflict right now by giving those who long for Kairi a bit of power and some people to rule over."

I shudder. "You sound like Takanori."

Saki shrugs.

"What? You don't mind sounding like Takanori?" Sometimes Saki, the Maymuan from Mu, returns and I don't like her.

"You want to be so unlike Takanori that you risk being nothing," Saki snaps.

I don't know what to say. She continues. "There can be no void, Kaori. It is like the shell – when it is extinguished we have to get rid of it before something tries to reside inside."

"Well, that's not a good example because I don't get rid of the shells anymore. You are as mad as those still stinging themselves now that Kairi's gone. It is over. Mu has gone. All those rituals and ways are gone."

"The island is no more but it lives inside many still," Saki says.

In the gloss of her eyes I see Mu as she was – beautiful, perched on the turquoise sea, waves lapping her shore. Pure. Except for us – the impure; undeserving of paradise. Naho would say there is no pure and impure land. Only our minds.

These thoughts are making red ants crawl under my skin. “I need to see Ren. Now.”

The garden blooms with roses – pink, red, and white, pistils exposed. I resist their intoxicating scent and run to my son.

“Where is Ren?”

Ren’s chamber is littered with discarded scrolls, illegible scrawled glyphs, and carved wooden figures. The tutor looks up in surprise. She glances around the chamber as if looking for an errant fly, not my beautiful son.

“Where is he?” I scream, and she scrambles to her feet, her scarred arm exposed as her sleeve flaps.

“I’m not sure,” she says, looking around again, hopeful he will reappear. “He must be with Eri. You know what those two are like.”

The tutor is confused by my glare. She looks to Saki, who gives a barely perceptible head shake. I grunt in frustration and sweep from the chamber. This temple is full of useless people.

“Is everything okay?” the tutor calls after us.

I push hard and the door to my chamber crashes against the wall. Eri drops her broom.

He is not here. I turn on Saki.

"Don't look at me like that! I have no idea where he is," Saki says, raising her palms in surrender.

Eri and Saki stare as my eyes dart around, searching for something to smash in frustration.

"Here," Eri says and hands me the pot of crushed galena. I squeeze the clay and Eri has such a curious, expectant expression that I almost laugh.

"Thank you," I say and gently return the pot to the table. "Will you help me find him?"

"Yes," Eri says simply.

"We have looked in every chamber in this ratty pyramid. Where is he?" My palms are sweating and the urge to punch through a wall is returning.

Saki squints and walks over to look through a slit overlooking the courtyard. "He must be outside."

"We *were* outside. We would have seen him," I snap.

"He *could* be outside," Eri whispers.

Beyond the slit, a vulture screams.

"You cannot go outside again," Saki says, trying to hold my arm.

I shake her off. I run down the stone steps of the temple and sprint across the stone-walled courtyard. A scarred guard stands at the gate.

"Open," I command and the gate creaks back to reveal a bustling marketplace.

I spin on the spot and frantically look for the tight black curls of my son, but all I see are more and more shocked faces as my presence is noted.

A soft hand tugs mine.

"There he is." Eri points.

Leaning against the outer courtyard wall, scrawling glyphs in the sand with a large black feather, is Ren. And Takafumi.

"What do you think you are doing?" I hiss, rushing over to them.

Takafumi surveys us with a calm expression. "We are practising glyphs."

"Look, Mumu."

Ren smiles a wide-toothed grin and pokes the sandy glyph with his feather.

I snatch Ren up and he writhes and screams, "No, Mumu, no."

"Shut up! Get inside now," I hiss.

Ren screams louder and wriggles from my grip. He lands with a thud and, crying, crawls towards Takafumi, who embraces him.

"Ren, please come here." I squat and open my arms but he snuggles further into Takafumi. I feel the eyes of the market burning through us and my legs begin to shake. I turn to Saki, who is watching in horror. Eri steps forward and holds out her hand to Ren. He toddles to her, panting, trying to catch his breath, his face flushed from crying.

"Don't forget your feather," Takafumi says and Ren snatches the feather and allows Eri to lead him back through the gate into the temple.

My legs buckle and I stumble to my knees. I look at what Ren has written in the sand. It is the glyph for fire.

All that has been burning inside me for so long explodes and I claw at the glyph with my fingernails until the sand turns to waves.

A shocked mutter ripples through the market.

I stand and kick the sand at Takafumi. He carefully dusts off his robe, turns away, and is swallowed by the stalls.

"Let's go," Saki says.

I glance at my people and they stare back in horror at my rage.

THREE

Takafumi

Blackland – Orbit Four

The message comes after the sun has crashed into the land – about a woman trapped in a restless sleep. A fever ripping through their village.

Takafumi holds the memory of Kaori raging in the market tight in his palm, burning like a bloodstone.

Ren's tiny embrace ensures the dream of the Kai is alive. The boy is Kaori's greatest weakness. If Takafumi can earn his allegiance, the Kai will rally around a new leader. One with a direct bloodline of Kairi. A pure he.

Takafumi and two members of the Kai arrive at a hut far beyond the shadow of Kaori's pyramid. The door, formed from tightly woven crow feathers, glistens in the moonlight.

The door swings open. "There is not long now," an

old man says, allowing Takafumi to enter the hut. The Kai remain stationed outside.

"Here she is." He gestures reluctantly to a woman sprawled on the floor.

Takafumi looks into her feverish eyes.

She is dying. Already her skin has taken on the waxy pallor of those already gone. He looks at her neck – the skin is thin, with no comfort for her brittle bones. This will not be difficult. The long sword dangling from the rope beneath his cloak taps his leg as he approaches her.

"Experienced Takanori," she gasps, gazing into Takafumi's face.

Takafumi grimaces. It hurts to be mistaken for the former leader of the Experienced. If Kaori had only extinguished the volcano and not flooded the island, life could have continued on Mu and Takafumi would have been the natural heir to Takanori's throne. Instead, Takanori is dead, Kairi has fled, and here Takafumi is trying to keep some semblance of the Mu rituals alive in this dreadful sandpit, surrounded by people obsessed with Kairi.

He had made the decision after Kaori had split the sky and created the Nile; best to try and harness the loyalty to Kairi but use the mask of the Experienced to secure a place in Kaori's temple. Whatever happened, he would never accept a society built by a carrier. He would never accept Kaori. But he would certainly use her son.

"Is there anyone else here?" Takanori asks, peering around the candlelit hut.

"No," says the old man, "I made sure of it. Just us."

Takafumi surveys him. His tired brown robe hangs loose on strong shoulders – he must have had constructing duty on Mu. His arm has the scars of the Kai and his eyes blaze, unflinching, before Takafumi's stare. He is capable of doing what needs to be done.

Takafumi gestures to the two men outside the hut. "They will take her shell."

The old man bites down hard on his lip but agrees. Silence falls. He kneels down beside the woman and takes her hand. "She was my pair. We made four for the island… Namu May Mu."

"She has seen many orbits for a carrier. You are a true Maymuan and the island honours your fulfilled duty," Takafumi says. He removes his cloak and the man grimaces at the sword.

"This is from Mu – it was in one of Kairi's stolen pods," Takafumi says, but the man's piety does not run to being grateful for Maymuan butchery.

"When?" the man asks, unable to take his eyes from the sword. Speckles of candlelight dance on the blade, careful not to linger too long.

"Now," Takafumi says.

The man's eyes dart around the hut, searching for a reason to prolong the moment of mercy, to share more time with his pair. "She has been saying things ... about Mu."

Takafumi resists the urge to roll his eyes. It was often like this. Anything to avoid the inevitable. "Of course she has. She should be there. We all should if not for cockroach Kaori."

The man's eyes narrow. "I would never let the pyramid take her. It is wicked what they do."

Takafumi nods slowly. It was unbelievable. How could Kaori have been so ignorant?

The news had spread like swamp roots… Kaori was not destroying the shells of the dead. She couldn't have given the Kai a better gift. Takafumi had decided he had to see for himself, and what he saw over an orbit ago still soured his stomach.

Beneath the main chamber the dead lay. She had stolen all that was soft and alive before interring them – the heart, intestines, and eyes cut out with a precision more terrifying than any frenzied attack. She then scented and oiled the skin with herbs and spices as if about to roast the flesh over a pit and consume it. And then – it still made Takafumi retch to think of it – she wrapped them. Again and again, tighter and tighter, until their wrists stuck to their hips. Even the face. Wrapped.

He'd had to leave after that – he still wasn't sure where she then moved them. Stacked, most likely. And now, every time he has to be in the main chamber, he thinks of them. The Maymuans piled up beneath their feet. Unable to escape.

It was and is wrong, and so he will continue to do everything he can to ensure the Kai receive a true Maymuan end.

Takafumi kneels beside the woman. "Namu May Mu."

"Namu May Mu," she rasps in delight.

"Namu Kai," Takafumi says.

The woman peers at him in confusion.

"Namu Kai," the man says and strokes the woman's scarred hand.

"Is it time for the Preparers?" The woman's gaunt face cracks with delight. "It should be boar today!"

Takafumi and the man exchange a glance.

"Yes," the man says, and the woman struggles to sit up. "Don't worry. I will bring it to you. You rest here with Takafumi."

"Who?" the woman asks.

The man scrunches his eyes together so tears cannot fall.

Takafumi raises his palms flat in prayer. "Eternal Maymuan, of the earth, sky, and sea. May the earth embrace you. Namu May Mu. May the sky surround you. Namu May Mu. May the sea guide you. Namu May Mu."

The woman sits bolt upright as if struck by lightning.

"Rest, my love, please." The man tries to push her to the floor, but her back will not bend.

"Takanori!" she screams.

Takafumi seizes her by the shoulders and also tries to push her to the floor, but even with the two men struggling she cannot be controlled.

"It is coming. It is coming," she says.

The men let go.

"The split. It is coming. Split again."

Takafumi shivers. She must be talking about the twins, Kaori and Kairi.

"One will rise, and never be forgotten. The other will fall, betrayed by their own flesh."

The woman collapses then, exhausted, and lands with a dull thud on the dusty floor. Her eyelids close and she relaxes, as if immediately entering a beautiful dream.

The man reaches for Takafumi's sword. "Do it. Do it now."

The sword trembles in Takafumi's hand.

"Please," pleads the man.

Takafumi tries to gather his thoughts. The sword weighs heavy in his palm. Betrayed by their own flesh? Does she mean Ren betraying Kaori? Takafumi shivers with exhilaration.

The man tugs on Takafumi's robe. "Please! She is going."

The woman's chest heaves as death rattles her ribcage.

With an almighty swing Takafumi strikes the woman.

The cave is empty. There are no crowds this night to eat his robe or soothe his wound.

Takafumi ignites the fire pit in the corner and gently places the woman's head with the others. A few have almost become skulls but most are still to decompose. The fire warms the stench of decay.

Takafumi knows the man would have preferred her to have a sky burial but it is too exposed.

The Kai burn and the man will have to take peace from the dark smoke smouldering in the desert and trust his pair has been returned to the sky.

FOUR

Kaori

Blackland – Orbit Four

Bees nestle in the exposed yellow heart of the blue lotus. Their stingers scratch the swaying stamen but nothing can deter the flower from blooming.

Ren kicks the side of my chair. Again.

"Eri?"

Eri wanders over, milk jug still in hand. She gives Ren his wooden toy, a particularly cruel-looking cat someone in the temple has carved for him. I don't appreciate his love of cats. They attack my snakes, which seems to be the reason everyone likes them so much. Ren throws the cat across the room then lies on his back and screams at the ceiling.

"Stop it, Ren!" I shout.

Eri is torn between continuing to fill my milk bath and rescuing my son from my temper.

I don't need this. The Blacklanders are already assembled on the banks of the Nile for the blue lotus ceremony, waiting for me to flood the ratty thing. If I don't, the soil beyond the banks will be barren for an orbit and we won't be able to grow enough food to feed us all. It is exhausting to think about it. I haven't bathed yet, let alone fixed my hair and skin glyphs.

"Where is Saki?" I bark at Eri.

"I don't know." She scuttles to pick up the cat toy. "Should I go and find her?"

"Yes," I hiss.

Eri hands Ren the toy and gently strokes the top of his head. He almost purrs. But as soon as the door slams behind her he is screaming again. I stare at him. His screams fill my chamber and I take a strange comfort from the familiar feeling of panic it brings to my chest.

It reminds me of Mu. Constant dread. Each cry tries to drag me closer but I lean further away from my son. The scorch of panic rises up through my shoulders and my neck burns.

"Mumu!" Ren wails.

I watch him, arms raised to me, tears and spit soaking his tunic. My tongue begins to tingle and swell and raw heat burns my cheeks. I want to lie in my bath. I want Eri to comb my hair. I want to appear perfect in front of the assembled Blacklanders. But this little beast won't let me.

"Mumu!" Ren screams, panic also now in his voice.

It strikes me like a poisoned arrowhead. "I'm sorry, I'm sorry, I'm sorry."

I scoop him up and he burrows as close as he can into my chest. I sit down and cuddle him and soon his eyes close and we breathe together.

Saki enters with Eri and her lovely face breaks into a contented smile. She comes and embraces us both. I glance at Eri and she quickly turns from my gaze and busies herself with filling the bath.

"We are so lucky, aren't we?" Saki says, enjoying the scent of Ren's hair.

"Yes," I mumble, thankful she did not walk in five steps earlier.

Ren stirs at the sound of Saki's voice and she takes my place cuddling him. I remove my robe and sink into the milk bath. The sweet fleshy smell of freshly drawn milk is an escape. I sink further into the bath until Eri hurries over and holds my hair high above the milk. Saki tuts, "Really? Everyone is waiting for you."

I know, but Saki doesn't understand what it takes to flood the Nile. To feel my hair drenched in the warm milk is not too much to ask. I twist from Eri's grip and splash into the depths of the bath.

Two sly orange snake eyes greet me. I have returned

to the belly of the snake that swallowed me whole in the prophesy chamber of the Experienced temple. I feel safe here.

Blink.

I miss you too.

"Oh Kaori!" Saki shouts.

I resurface with a sudden lurch, soaking the floor. Ren has crawled from her and is joyfully smacking his palms on the soiled ground. I giggle, watching Ren, but the sound dies in my mouth when I realise Eri is ready to cry.

"It's okay. I'll rinse it myself," I say, knowing Eri will have to wash my hair.

I clamber out of the bath and Saki tosses me a robe. "Get ready," she hisses through clenched teeth. "I'll find someone to clean this now or we'll never get the smell out." She gives me a final glare, scoops Ren up, and storms out, slamming the door.

"Look, she's made even more mess," I say, pointing at the milky footsteps forming a trail behind Ren. "It will be all over the temple now."

Eri does not respond and works on soaking as much milk from my hair into a cloth as she can.

I wrap my fingers around her wrist. "It's okay."

Her lip trembles.

I smile. "I promise it's okay. There's time." She finally

uncoils a little. "Anyway, there is no ceremony without me. They can wait."

Takafumi will enjoy the extra time without my presence. He has been unbearable since the market incident – and Ren won't settle without that ratty feather. I threw it away but he was so hysterical we had to find another one. Turns out it was from a crow that only nests on the other side of the desert. Typical Takafumi. Has to have his own secret little things – his little trinkets. It's pathetic.

My chamber door creaks open when Ren and Saki return.

"Mumu wow!" Ren says.

I raise an eyebrow at Saki and she surveys me from head to toe, her eyes shining. "Mumu wow indeed."

I stand in the middle of the room, transformed into the leader of Blackland. I am their leader. What I want doesn't matter. After creating the Nile, the people, scarred or otherwise, recognised my power. They saw with their own eyes my ability to create. And they already knew my capacity to destroy. The island of Mu collapsed within one rise. Saki made it as clear as water in a lagoon. It is either you they will follow or the

Experienced. Until the final Experienced takes their final breath I have no choice but to lead.

And we all depend on water to survive.

There came a time when even the Nile was not enough. Two orbits ago we needed another source of food beyond the banks of the Nile, but the packs sent to find any edible vegetation or meat could not cross the desert before their water bags ran dry. They all returned delirious with thirst. I sneaked out at night when the air was still moist. I rode a camel. In the temple, the Experienced had started to turn their rumbling stomachs to the one hump, but they are far more useful for milk and to explore the desert. The ebb and flow of their gait reminded me of navigating the pod across the ocean to Blackland. I sailed the desert waiting for the tinkle of water in my veins, but I could feel nothing but the scratch of the sand on my skin. Just a bit further, I thought. But still nothing, only the crunch beneath hooves and a creeping heat as the stars faded to welcome the sun. I should have returned to the temple when the moon no longer lit our path and we witnessed a darkness known only to those able to endure and wait for the light. It burned the back of my neck first, then the tips of my fingers. Even my white robes, wrapped as if shrouding the dead, could not keep the heat out. I dripped the last of my water bag into my mouth and still did not return. *I must be close. I can't feel anything wrapped up like this,* I thought. I unwrapped my robe from my face and peered into the horizon.

I only closed my eyes for a moment but woke sprawled on the camel's neck. I tried to sit up and catch my breath but it slipped through my fingers and slid down the side of the camel. I chased it and I landed with a thud on the sand. The heat beneath and above drew the last moisture from my shell. I rolled to the only darkness I could find: the shadow cast by the camel. I don't know how long I lay beside the camel. I stared into the cloudless sky. Sand filled my mouth as a warm wind smeared my face with the desert. I was sinking. He was relentless in his pursuit, strong and ruthless; pinning me to the floor and methodically burying my shell alive.

Until she came. A crescent moon. Black against the deep-blue sky. I opened my mouth and she dropped it from her beak. A snail. I chewed the slime and crunched the shell until I was able to sit up in the shadow of the camel and greet my friend – shrewd dark eyes, strong black neck, pure white feathers and a proud black tail: the ibis. She stabbed my hand with the tip of her long beak and then shoved it into the sand. Again, she stabbed and dipped. Her glossy eyes bored into me. Wet and shiny. *Water*. I plunged my hand into the hole created by her beak until my shoulder slammed the sand. Then I withdrew my arm, but it was dry. The ibis glared. I plunged two arms into the sand

and dug deeper. Again they returned dry. The ibis surveyed the well I had made and shoved her face in the hole, burrowing deeper. She then resurfaced and faced me. The tip of her beak glistened. I gasped because the chill of fresh water shivered through my soul. I shoved my face in the well and, in one mighty stream, water erupted from the earth. I lay on my back and laughed as cool, fresh water soaked both the sand and my robes.

Now my skin shines not from water but with the oil of crushed seeds from the garden. My hair is braided in glossy twists woven with gold. My ceremonial robe is a long golden dress. Across my shoulder lies a wide collar as blue and magnificent as the sea and around my waist is a matching obi knotted in the shape of an ankh. Eri has meticulously drawn glyphs on my arms. Every glyph we have for water is etched down my arm.

Ren runs to me and both Saki and Eri scream, "No!"

I pick him up and he smears the glyph on my upper arm. Saki and Eri make to snatch him from me but I hold him tight.

"I am proud to wear the glyph of my son."

I look at the smudged ink.

"And of my love." I hold out my other arm to Saki.

She sighs but extends her index finger and carefully smudges the glyph on my forearm.

Saki takes Ren. I turn to Eri. "And of you, too."

I hold out the back of my hand to Eri. She looks at Saki, who smiles at her and nods with encouragement.

Eri gently runs her nail across the glyph on my hand. "What does it feel like?" she whispers.

I look at her in surprise.

"The water, what does it feel like?" she asks again, slightly breathless.

To hold eternity in the palm of my hand? To enter the infinite and roll and splash within? To know what opens a bud, what soars beneath a wing? It feels like a secret we share, but the final glyph was given to me and me alone. No one else will truly understand.

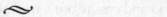

The banks of the Nile are packed full of Blacklanders when we arrive. I'm pleased to see there is a mix of white robes and brown robes.

The air hums with anticipation as I take my place on the newly erected platform overlooking the river. Saki sits beside me, gorgeous in a bright white robe, her gold beads swaying from the end of her long braids. A wooden archway heavy with intricately sewn white roses and white lilies soars overhead. On either side is a large basin full of water where sprawled blue lotuses bob, their yellow centres soaking up the last of the sun.

I bow in greeting to the assembled leaders, including

Takafumi. He bows swiftly in return, which is odd because he has been taking every opportunity to smirk ever since I destroyed the fire glyph. At least I know where Ren is right now; in my chamber with Eri and under strict orders not to put even one toe outside of the door until I return from the ceremony.

I straighten and the hum of the crowd becomes a roar. I raise my arms to the sun, which still rests high in the sky before it begins its dusk descent.

My name flits across the Nile.

"Namu Kaori," they chant. Not all, I expect. I am not close enough to see individual mouths but there is enough noise to fill me with the energy needed to flood the land and ensure our survival.

I drop my arms and silence falls.

Below, the lotuses are released. The dark water of the Nile becomes bright blue as the lotus flowers sail serenely. The sun begins its red descent and scroll lanterns are gently pushed out onto the water to play with the petals. Together they dance and are soon joined by golden fireflies that flit from the heart of the lotus to the soul of the flame.

I reach out to hold Saki's hand. We watch the lanterns caress the Nile. I take a sip of blue wine and entwine my fingers with hers. When this is all over, I look forward to making love with her under the moon.

The crowds gasp as my snakes break the surface to

peer at the crowds, curious about all the activity so close to their home. A pair of orange eyes blinks again in my mind. Ever since Saki cut me from the enormous snake on Mu I have become their kin. I feel them the same way I can feel water in my veins. I am them. And here in Blackland I am grateful their loyalty extends beyond Mu. Their long necks undulate, nudging the lotus, and I rise to greet them.

A steep staircase descends from the platform and a wide path lined by guards guides me to the dark water. I descend. I walk the narrow dirt path to the Nile and scuffles break out amongst the Blacklanders beyond the guards. I ignore them because I have to focus on the river. Thankfully I only have to push the water over one bank today. Later, when this side is no longer full of people, I will return.

Long, thick black snakes slither out of the river and meet me halfway up the path. They coil around my legs, waist, and neck, and I enjoy their constriction. I hurry to the water's edge but before I can enter, the snake around my neck squeezes tight and twists. I turn to alleviate the pressure and a familiar set of eyes locks on to mine. I recognise the rage. It is the smith who was kicked out of the main chamber. The snake hisses and lunges at him.

"No!" I shout and seize hold of its tail.

The smith does not flinch. He narrows his eyes and hurls something at me.

I step back but nothing strikes. Instead, a black feather floats through the air between us. I watch it gently traverse the air and land softly on the grass. I look to the smith but he has gone, swallowed by the crowd crushing forward to see why I have not yet entered the water.

What was that about?

I look back up the staircase for Saki but I cannot see her lovely face from here.

I don't know what to do. I stand, struck dumb for a moment, then a snake brings its face to mine, hisses, and bares it fangs in warning.

Wake up.

I can't just stand here.

I quickly enter the water. The cold soaks the hem of my dress, and when my knees are submerged I can almost forget the incident with the feather completely.

I close my eyes and let the Nile flood my veins. She courses through my shell. I can't flood the bank until I feel whole. I have been told for far too many orbits that I am a half. I am incomplete. I need my twin.

I reach into the pocket of my dress. There it is. The stone that fell from Aito's dying mouth.

Kairi's bloodstone.

The green stone throbs in my hand. The red flecks across the stone burn my palm. I see Kairi swirling defiantly down into the depths of my whirlpool. We lock eyes and the elements of fire and water pierce through eternity.

Here on Blackland, waves churn the Nile. The lotus petals flee as though in panic. The snakes weave around my feet as wave after wave crashes over the lush land already watered by the Nile and pours over the dry, thirsty desert beyond.

I return to my throne on the platform, relieved that Saki and the ibis can take over. The magnificent bird rests on a long wooden raft towed by a lone boat. Dusk has fallen. Lanterns burn around the raft, illuminating the ibis's flawless white torso. Its long, sharp, curved beak looms over the water. Saki sits, safe in the boat, her white robe fluttering as she gently rows the ibis across the now calm Nile. My snakes circle them, rippling the water and nudging the raft along the bank before the crowd.

I idolise the ibis because she was a crescent moon ascending when I was in the depths of despair in the desert.

"Namu ibis," I whisper, then I hear a sound I haven't heard since we were back on Mu; the spit of an arrow from a bow. We don't use bows and arrows here. If you must kill then you must also look and bear witness to the sacrifice. There are no coward kills on Blackland.

Spit. Spit. Spit.

Then the earth trembles as the crowds flee.

It feels like Kairi is trying to throw us all off the land again, but I know that can't be possible.

Countless feet pound the sand and the whole platform shudders. The flower arch sways violently and I watch as a trail of white robes sprints towards the temple.

Saki.

I push against the tide and tumble down the staircase and along the abandoned path. The raft and boat have crashed on the side and I can't see Saki anywhere.

I finally reach the raft and see that white has become red.

The ibis is dead.

Long black-feathered arrows pierce its white breast and blood oozes from its wounds, staining its plume.

Terror seizes my heart. Where is Saki?

I approach the boat next. I can't yet see inside but my stomach churns as I recognise the shape of protruding arrow tails. The image of Saki's white robe soaked in red like the ibis flashes through my mind.

All is black in the boat. Snakes lie slain, arrows stuck in their beautiful black scales. They are coiled around her, protecting my love, giving their life for hers – as I would.

I unwrap the snakes and find Saki unconscious beneath them. I scoop her up into my arms and dip her gently in the water. She wakes with a splutter.

"What?" she mumbles, confused.

"Tell me what happened, Saki. What did you see?"

"I–I don't know… Where am I?" She sits up and then screams when she sees the ibis. "Oh, Kaori, *no.*" I hold her close as she sobs. "What is this?"

We look at the arrows jutting out of the snakes like cracked bone through skin.

"I was rowing," Saki says, "and then it was as if the air had been snatched from my lungs. I couldn't breathe at all."

They saved her.

Before the arrows could find their target, the snakes left the Nile and constricted her – shielded her.

The boat begins to rock as my rage makes the water writhe.

Inside the temple there is chaos.

Saki and I run past the commotion to my chamber. Ren is sitting alone and looks up with delight at our return. He is oblivious to the danger outside. He is playing with his wooden toys but Eri is nowhere to be seen.

I look around the chamber but there is no sign of a struggle.

"Ren," I say, crouching to see my son, "where is Eri?"

"Eri!" he replies, beaming, and looks to the door as if she is about to enter.

Saki and I exchange a glance. *Where the ratty hell is she?* I hope she's okay.

The chamber door bursts open and Ren's tutor staggers in. "Go! You have to go." She runs and grabs Saki. "I am so glad you're okay. They said you had been killed! You must go. *All* of you. It is not safe here."

"What's happening?" Saki asks. I scoop Ren up but he wriggles back to the floor and his toys.

The tutor stares at him with fear. "They are saying it is the followers of Kairi. The Kai, they call themselves."

I shudder. The bloodstone in my pocket burns.

"Where is Eri?" I ask. The tutor looks as if I have lost my mind.

"Eri? She has gone. She has the scars like me. It is not safe for those like us either, we who are not the Kai but who share the skin. They're ripping each other apart in the market. It doesn't matter if they say they follow you or not. The scar is enough to warrant an attack."

I slump into my chair and stare at the galena pot.

"Where will she have gone?" I ask. Now Saki also looks at me with ill-disguised disgust.

"Who cares, Kaori? Did you hear? They are *raging* outside!" Saki shrieks.

I leap from the chair. "So what? We should just leave

her? She is not part of this Kai thing. You know that as well as I do!"

"*Look,*" Saki shouts, "look at our son! They want to hurt him. And you. They almost *killed* me!"

The tutor's neck swivels, mouth ajar at our exchange. She casts a fearful look over her shoulder at the door. The sounds of angry voices ricochet down the hall and seem to physically bang on the door.

"If we let these Kai terrorise us then they have won," I hiss. "They want terror. They want us to abandon all that we value. If I let Eri leave here without fighting for her return then I may as well hand them the temple now."

Saki shakes her head violently. The beads from her braids jangle against her neck. "No. How do you know she hasn't been working with them?"

I grunt in frustration. "Saki, you are letting them win. Stop. Find yourself."

Tears fall from Saki's eyes – from rage or despair, I do not know.

She grabs the galena pot and squeezes it in her fist. She is scared. I understand fear.

But here is Kairi again, blazing through my land, scorching all that he sees.

No. I hate this ratty sandpit but he is *not* taking what is mine. And how can I save all if I am afraid to rescue one?

"I am going to get Eri," I say and cover my robes with a brown cloak. I close the door behind me and the crack of the galena pot smashing against the door sets Ren wailing.

Two orbits ago when I sneaked out to find a source of water, I passed the settlement where most of the scarred reside.

I have never been in amongst their huts though, so now I pull my dark cloak tight and conceal my face as best I can. The huts are not as neat as the ones we built on Mu. Some are lopsided and clearly built only with what could be foraged. My cheeks burn with shame at my ignorance of what has been happening right outside my temple.

It is strange to think of Eri here. I am so used to seeing her with the beauty of the Nile as a backdrop outside my chamber or in the light shining in Ren's eyes. I can feel water here but it is rancid. Puddles of stagnant water purr with flies and glisten with rotten food. Discarded pieces of fish bone are fought over by hungry, cawing crows.

A face peers from an opening. I approach quickly, holding the cloth of my hood carefully over my mouth and nose as I ask, "Do you know Eri?" I find my tongue catches on her name and I swallow the emotion. "She is a little shorter than me and has hair braided from the temple with gold beads?" The stranger takes a long, hard look and a finger extends and points to a hut at the end of the row.

I hurry over to it.

"Hello? Eri?" I call into the dark opening. People rustle inside. A large man appears. He surveys my dark cloak and casts a shrewd look over the hood concealing my hair. He stares into the only exposed part of my shell: my eyes.

"Who are you?" he barks.

"I am looking for Eri. She is needed in the temple," I say.

The Blacklander laughs and sneers, "There won't be a temple by the next rise."

I shiver.

"Eri is needed."

There is a scuffle at the opening and Eri stumbles out. Her eyes lock on mine and she gasps.

"Get back inside," the Blacklander says gruffly. Eri tries to step further out. The man turns and for a moment I am afraid he is going to strike her, but instead he strokes her hair with tenderness and says softly, "Go in, Eri. It is over. You don't need to be with them anymore. We are free."

Eri looks at me in panic.

"Don't worry, we will get rid of whoever this is now and make sure they know never to return here," he says, snarling at me. He pushes Eri back into the hut and Eri's carrier appears holding a baby.

"Go away," she says. "This is your last chance. We don't want anyone from the temple here."

I can feel the eyes of more Blacklanders peeking in from the opening but I can't move. The baby. Its probing gaze bores into mine.

"Go!" Eri's carrier shouts, and shifts the baby to her other arm.

Ocean-deep cold water drips down my spine and I let go of the cloth covering my mouth. The baby has a scarred arm. The thought of the agony of the lash on such pure skin trembles my knees. I could vomit. I pull the cloth back over my mouth and retch.

"Wait!" the woman shouts. "Eri. Eri! Quick, come here. Who is this? Do you recognise her?"

I back away but stumble over those who have left their huts for a closer look.

"Someone grab her!" Eri's carrier shouts.

A firm hand seizes my elbow. I spin to face my attacker and find myself in the clutches of Takafumi.

He stares but does not confirm my identity.

"I will take this back to the temple."

And before anyone can protest, he drags me out of their village.

FIVE

Takafumi

Blackland – Orbit Four

A warm wind rustles the iridescent black feathers of the arrow. Takafumi runs his hand up the wooden shaft to the sharp tip.

"Beautiful," he murmurs before returning it to the large pile.

Members of the Kai continue to work: pounding metal; shaving bark; plucking feathers. Preparing for war.

A tall, lean man approaches Takafumi. His muscles strain beneath his taut skin. His entire shell, including his face and shaved head, is covered in scars.

"Takafumi," he says in greeting, and bows deeply.

Takafumi looks into the dark eyes now fixed upon him.

"Junta," Takafumi says to the commander of the Kai, "I am so glad to finally be able to greet you in the open." Junta nods graciously. Takafumi continues, "I am grateful for all you have done. The attack on the ceremony was a success."

Takafumi watches Junta's face carefully for any glimpse of vulnerability, like a hungry spider lurking in a shadow. He never agreed with Takanori's relentless whip. He lures instead with honeycomb so those he ensnares don't realise the sweetness is hiding poison until it's far too late.

Junta steps onto Takafumi's sticky web. "I did not succeed," Junta snarls with a scowl. "Saki is still alive."

"We all underestimated the snakes," Takafumi says evenly. If Junta was to stop scowling at the sand, he would see the true fury in Takafumi's face.

"Yes," Junta says. "But a fatal blow was delivered. They can ignore us no more. When will you join us?"

Takafumi frowns. "I already lead you."

"Yes. Takafumi, I didn't mean to imply—" Takafumi raises his hand for the young man to be quiet. Junta has the skin of Kairi but not the soul. He is no renegade. He wants to follow, not lead.

"Now is not the time," Takafumi says, looking beyond Junta to the many members of the Kai. They sit in packs in the shadow of the skull cave, doing all they can to prepare for the fall of the temple. Cruel spears jut from the sand. Knives glisten in the sun. Bows quiver with arrows eager to pierce the unprepared. This first attack was too chaotic. After Junta failed to kill Saki, Blacklanders who were not initiated into the Kai began to riot and a methodical attack became impossible. Takafumi lost Kaori in the chaos so the Kai must now bide their time before striking again. "She does not yet know I am the leader of the Kai. I can still roam the temple… And she is weak."

He felt it – the brittleness of her ribcage as he held her while she sobbed. It scared her, to see her land as it is. The injustice. The rage. To realise her gilded chamber is really a cage. And now the cage has been rattled. He knows Kaori felt trapped before, but she thought the walls were trying to keep the Kai out, not keep her in. And now it is too late.

She will never unite Blackland and Redland. Those loyal to Kairi will never forgive her for stealing their destiny. They don't want to be ruled by a carrier. Kaori represents the drowning of their beloved island along with the predictability of order and hierarchy. There needs to be a figure who reconciles the split Maymuans. Who represents both a memory and a hope for the future.

Only the boy, Ren, can do that.

SIX

Kaori

Blackland – Orbit Four

The temple did not fall. It was shaken, rattled, but it still stands. The night of the ibis will haunt my dreams for many moons – maybe for the rest of my orbits – but I will not let it undo me. I can't. I promised myself I would find a safe land for Ren far from the cruelty of Mu.

Takafumi and I returned to the temple to find Blacklanders fighting each other. Brown robes versus white robes; those from outside the temple attacking those who dwell within. It seemed more frenzied and random than the attack on Saki. Less coordinated. Not so much the Kai as angry Blacklanders taking their frustrations out on the temple. In the chaos I lost Takafumi so I hurried straight to my secret hiding place, where the scarred are afraid to venture; the corpse chamber below the main hall.

I don't share their fear. I find comfort in knowing my shell will be preserved, not maimed and fed to the predators in the sky like the innocent unnamed sacrificed on Mu.

Saki was crouching behind the embalming table with Ren.

"What is happening?" Saki asked.

Ren peeled himself from Saki and dived into my arms. "Mumu, I'm scared."

Even now the memory of Ren's fear makes my skin tingle. I was so angry at the Blacklanders for destroying their own temple. And as for the Kai, I wanted to drown every single one of them for the turmoil they had brought to Blackland.

Saki insisted I remain below ground until the roof was no longer rumbling with the rioters above. I know in my role as leader it is my duty to survive, but I felt so pathetic to be burrowed underground while innocent people were being attacked above.

When there was finally no sound to be heard from above, we emerged into the main temple. Maimed shells lay scattered across the main hall. Ren, mercifully, had fallen asleep and was sheltered in my arms.

The thrones Saki and I sit on during meetings had been looted and I later discovered every violated chamber had possessions looted too. The walls were ablaze with scrawled fire glyphs. We had to dedicate a chamber to treat the injured. There was immediate conflict between me and the furious temple dwellers who wanted to kick out any injured scarred Blacklanders, but how could I ask for unity and then begin restoring the temple with division? We treated all injured in the same chamber.

I was grateful to Takafumi and the Experienced, who rallied together to restore the temple.

Seven rises have passed since, and the rebellion wave has crashed; the water is now eerily calm. We are searching for members of the Kai but no one is claiming membership. The only action I have is to interrogate all with scars but that would be another form of terror. The unscarred have a blood lust that I cannot satiate.

For the temple to run efficiently, the scarred and unscarred must work side by side, but the tension is palpable. Some scarred have not returned at all – Ren's tutor was treated for her injuries and since leaving the temple has not been seen. To my surprise, Eri did return. She refused to say what had happened with her carrier and the others, but she has made it clear she can never go back to her hut. Saki wanted to get rid of her and insisted we only have the unblemished in our chamber, but how can I ask Eri to leave when she has made the ultimate sacrifice to serve us?

In the meantime, I have returned to flood the other

bank of the Nile. I have to. It is my duty as leader of Blackland.

Here I am again with duty. I feel so far from love I don't know how I can ever find it again. *Duty*. Allocated roles. Pairings. I understand now more than I did then. Is it wrong to try and control them a little? How else will they obey? My snakes can't coil Saki, or Ren, every time there is an attack. How can I protect us all without order? Without rules?

But first we need food and shelter. We need water.

I enter the Nile. I can't even feel the chill on my legs. I run my hand across the surface and it ripples – but no more. I squeeze the bloodstone. Nothing.

I sit and rest on the reeds, my toes dipped in the water. A large green fish grazes my ankle. It has clusters of black spots across its gorgeous iridescent scales. After a little more swimming it rests just beneath the surface and lies still, its glassy eye blinking. I wonder what it's doing but then the clusters of black spots spread like overturned blue wine. Tiny holes appear in the sand and I realise other fish are rushing to feed on it. Soon there is more black than green.

Move.

You need to move.

I splash above the fish with my hand but still it remains, its glassy eye blinking. I can't bear this. The water settles and becomes a mirror, and I am reflected in its sheen. I see something unfamiliar, something I have never felt in water before: fear. Something brushes against my foot and I leap out of the river. Another large fish approaches and circles the prone green fish, waiting to strike.

I stumble as I back away from the bank. I lie on my back amongst the reeds and try to breathe. My skin prickles with goosebumps. The more I try and steady my breath the worse it becomes. I run my fingers through the reeds, desperate to feel anything other than fear. The blue sky above seems to tremble. I can't remain conscious – my fear is too great. I think of Saki, but I see her skewered with iridescent Kai arrows. I think of Ren, but I see him as the unnamed on the Experienced temple, his decapitated shell suspended. I scream and rip the reeds from the soil. My shell can no longer tolerate my racing heart. Black spots like the parasitic fish blur my vision. Fear consumes me.

SEVEN

Kairi

May - Orbit One

The pods lay exhausted on the shore. Ravenous Mayans had scattered in search of more than dried coco, deer and mango rations. They had entered the jungle, their hunger greater than their fear. Our new land welcomed us with an open palm and sprawled fingers. Tangled roots stretched across the beach, beckoning us into the dense, lush trees.

Kentaro stared into the dark heart of the jungle. What could he see? Our beginning or our end?

The low bushes trembled and Shun, Ikki, and Tetsu returned victorious with a squealing meal. It was some kind of boar. It had a similar face but instead of mud-encrusted bristles it had skin like a hippo. More packs emerged with the same animal, its curiosity our salvation. Sharpened gamgam from Mu pierced this new May creature's torso. Its blood quenched the thirst of all who had been stuck in those ratty pods for an almost unendurable number of moons.

Relentless rowing. The Mayans tucked in the honeycomb cells. Relentless buzzing. No silence. No escape.

Kentaro had been lucky. There had always been something for him to do to maintain the pod and ensure we didn't starve or drown. Without Ayana and the mayu, especially Kai, my shell would have arrived at May but my soul would have been lost to the moon – she, whose round flat face reappeared, calculating our time, then crept away crescent by crescent, only to return again, gloating at my incessant watery torment.

Some did lose their sanity during the journey, disturbing us all with their screams. I was disappointed that one of my pack succumbed to the taunt of the moon cycle. Tetsu began to screech at night like an owl closing in on its prey. Except Tetsu was inflicting this on himself – he was both hunter and prey. Kentaro and I decided to lock him and the other howlers down below with the oars. It certainly made the rowers row with more urgency.

On the beach, Mayans stacked piles of branches then struck their bloodstones with metal daggers to ignite a cooking fire. I paced the sand and enjoyed the familiar sensation of heat throbbing through my shoulders. Since the whirlpool, I hadn't felt a lick of flame. I can't create fire from nothing; I can only manipulate an existing flame. There was no reason to spark a bloodstone in the pod. So it was with relish that I flicked my finger at each pyre, creating even bigger flames, and soon the sweet, heady smell of roasting meat filled the air.

Hunger abated, at least for this rise, there was no inclination to explore our new land. They filed back into the pods and hid in the honeycomb. I ignited the shoreline between us and the jungle, but when we awoke the tide had deposited us into the lap of the trees and we could no longer avoid our fate.

The firepit in the centre of the jungle clearing flickers, illuminating the faces of the pod leaders. This natural clearing has become the centre of May. A place to plan, build, and, increasingly, a place for the pod leaders to whine and bleat like goats with rotten tongues about how ratty hard life is for them here.

"We just feel that without the foundation of the Experienced—" Matsu, one of the pod leaders, begins to say.

I hold up my hand and mercifully he stops. They say the same things every time we meet. There are no

Experienced here. Kaori took them with her. What do they want me to do? Sail for moons and go and pick them up? It is over.

"If we accept the loss of the Experienced," Matsu continues, "how are we supposed to overcome the absence of the rearers?"

This again! Pull the mayu out of the carriers, for ratty hell's sake. How hard can it be? Cut them out! Who cares, as long as the mayu survive.

Kentaro, who always sits beside me during these verbal ordeals, shifts uncomfortably. I don't need his nonsense now either. He may be my true love but he worries too much. It disturbs my mind.

"You need to think about how we are going to live together here. On Mu there was order. What is your order going to be?" Kentaro said soon after we arrived – and keeps saying now.

I don't know. I was so focused on penetrating the horizon I didn't consider beyond it. And now here we are. What is wrong with these Mayans? We couldn't have landed in a better place! The jungle is brimming with food, shelter, and opportunity.

"You need to focus all of your energy on building my temple," I say. The pod leaders exchange anxious glances. The only thing I agree with these parasites about is the need for a foundation. Not in terms of the Experienced, but May does need a core. A temple. My temple.

"We are building as fast as we can," Matsu says.

"If you spent less time trying to resuscitate Mu then it would be complete by now. Finish my temple and then we can work on what you ask."

Another anxious glance. I hate these gatherings.

"What do you want?" I ask. "There are no Experienced. There are no rearers."

None of the island duty packs are complete because she took half of them, for ratty hell's sake!

"I will not ask again. Tell me now. What. Do. You. Want?"

Silence.

One of the pod leaders, Goro, rises to his feet. "We want to be like you." Not only is his arm covered in scar tissue but his entire shell. Like mine. Goro continues, "We want to be free. Each pod is unique. We arrived at the same destination but we each had our own journey."

Well, that is ridiculous, but he is still going on.

"Let us forge our own path here. As your Mayans but with our own land and in whatever way we see best."

Kentaro grips tightly to my wrist. I flick him off. *Don't be so disturbed Ken-kun. It is only talk.* As if the pods could ever truly sever ties with me. I would burn their little settlements down. And they know it.

"Okay," I say, and Kentaro groans, stands up, and

walks away. "Finish my temple and you will have your freedom."

Kentaro is standing inside our temporary hut, waiting.

"Do you have any idea what you have given away?" He's so angry he's almost in tears.

"Calm down," I say. "It will get the temple finished, won't it? And then I will take it from there."

Kentaro screams in frustration. I stare at him. *Why is he so upset?*

"Even after the temple is finished, maybe you should give them what they asked for," a soft voice says. Closing our hut door carefully behind her is Ayana.

"Who invited you?" Kentaro snarls.

Ayana raises an eyebrow at me and I beckon her in. Kentaro begins pacing around the hut, rubbing his fist into his palm.

"I heard what happened at the pod leaders meeting," Ayana says.

Kentaro stops pacing and mutters, "Of course you did, you ratty snake."

Ayana and I ignore him, which sets him pacing again.

"What do you think?" I ask Ayana.

"I can't take any more of this," Kentaro says and

marches out, slamming the door. Our makeshift hut rattles.

A scowl briefly crosses Ayana's lovely, smooth face. "I think it could be good to have different villages"—she pauses—"centred around your temple of course. Then you will have the best of everything when they each excel in different areas."

Yes, I suppose so. I don't know. I want my ratty temple built.

"They were going on about your favourites again – the rearers," I tease, and a dark scowl falls and remains on Ayana's face. I laugh. "You hate them, don't you?"

Ayana blinks deeply and the scowl clatters to the floor, replaced with calm. "Like you hate the carriers?" she asks.

"I don't hate them. Not anymore. I don't hate you. You are a carrier."

"Not anymore," Ayana whispers.

I look at her properly. *Is she sad?*

"Is there someone you want to create with?" I ask and find I am holding my breath before her response.

"No. I told you. Kai is my last."

Good. I hate to admit it but I need Ayana. I can't explain it. I have wanted her by my side ever since she first appeared on my side of Mu, belly swollen with Kai, so eager to join May. Kai is the first pure Mayan. The first born on May beneath the shadow of the volcano I created to rip Mu apart. My infatuation with Ayana was so deep on Mu that I murdered her pair, Reo, so nothing and no one can ever come between us. I am glad she has not found another mate.

The silence between us allows the sound of Kentaro pacing around outside the hut muttering to himself to be heard.

"He is becoming…" I can't finish the sentence. I don't need to.

"He is not your only concern," Ayana whispers. "Tetsu is still not okay. I saw him carving the outline of a Mayan into the trunk of a tree by the shore. He was calling it Aito."

I shudder at the mention of his name. Aito. Another Maymuan I murdered. He may have been a member of my hunting pack on Mu but he had to be sacrificed. He was too close to my twin. I had to sever all his veins to provoke Kaori's rage and trigger a tsunami to get us off that ratty island.

Ayana continues, "And he was chanting 'Namu May Mu'."

For ratty hell's sake.

The door swings open.

"Are you two going to whisper to each other until the next rise or can I enter my own hut?" Kentaro spits, glaring at us.

Ayana smiles at Kentaro's jealousy and leans into me.

"Think carefully about the tribes, Kairi. It could be best to let them go."

I nod and watch her intentionally brush past Kentaro rather than wait for him to move.

"You need to be careful," Kentaro snarls, lurching towards me and poking me in my chest. "Remember, she was a water hunter before she was a carrier."

EIGHT

Kairi

May - Orbit Two

"Let them live in huts and we will live in stone," I explained to Kentaro, who still hasn't accepted the Mayans splitting off to form their own tribes. It is done. And now the most important thing is that my temple is complete.

It stands, magnificent, in the centre of the jungle, far from submerged Mu and even further from wherever Kaori landed with my stolen pods. Large stones were meticulously carved and hauled through the foliage to create the towering structure. On all four sides of the pyramid are tall staircases leading to a large chamber at the very top, which has replaced the clearing fire pit as our meeting place.

For the first few moons after the temple was

completed, the pod leaders would return and beg for what they needed to build their villages, but now after six moons they no longer do. Kentaro thinks it is dangerous to leave them unattended, but why should we care? We are the centre of the jungle and we have everything we need. I can reach up my hand and pluck fruit, dip my bag in the river and drink fresh water, lift the roots and feast on insects, or slit the throat of the beasts that roam and roast their flesh.

Now only my Mayans, the true Mayans who sailed in my pod, gather around the fire pit in the meeting chamber to tell tales and spin stories to entertain us all. There are a lot of carriers. I don't know how my pod ended up so full of them. But now they are not relentlessly trying to create maymu they have proven to be very skilled in hunting and gathering food and all the materials we need, not only to survive here but to thrive.

The fire pit crackles. Kentaro and I sit on an elevated platform and listen to the tales below. Kai rests on my lap. His beautiful eyes are closed, eyelashes soft against his plump cheek, and his chest rises and falls in a deep sleep. He can walk now. I love to watch him toddle around the base of the temple. Chubby hands clutch the stone steps and his halo of tight black curls wobbles. But something stirs inside me when I watch him sleep, when I watch his peace. It reminds me of playing with the rearers on the shore of Mu, during rises filled with collecting shells, slurping cocos, and nibbling spiders, when that was all I knew.

I shiver despite the heat of the pit and focus on the tale a she is telling which has the entire chamber's attention.

"When each of us are born, with our first breath we swallow a star. It burns inside. For those who understand the ebb and flow of this life, who embrace the tide, we can endure the pure flame. We know our only duty is to keep this gift pristine – sacred. It is the lantern that will guide our way, and to whom we will return when the eternal darkness falls. But there are those who can't endure their responsibility. They toss their star into the horizon. Splash. Purity lost." Then she gazes around the chamber, staring deep into the eyes of each Mayan. Her dark mane of hair has a spider's scrawl of silver at each temple. Her gaze locks on mine. "Now, the pitiful have a hole, scorched through by the star. They are condemned to wander this land and take what is not theirs to try and fill the space within. But nothing can replace the lost star."

Heat builds over my shoulders. I can't control my physical response to this disturbing tale. The need to manipulate fire churns my veins until my fingers flicker. The fire pit bursts into life with a roar and my flame licks the roof.

I hand Kai to Kentaro and step down from the

platform to confront this she. Why does she look so familiar?

"Who are you?"

She blinks slowly. "I am Miki."

Miki? I don't know why but she makes me think of Naho, even though her face is sharper and her eyes are much shrewder. I shudder.

"How do you get the star back?" Why has this Miki told such a ratty horrible story?

She looks at me and shrugs. "You can't."

"That doesn't make any sense. What is the point of this story?"

Miki watches me carefully. "I suppose we have to decide for ourselves what the meaning is." She pauses and looks into my flame, which is scorching the roof and turning the room into a furnace. "I believe we can only be reunited with our star in death after we have plunged the deepest ocean and retrieved it."

I stare at her and feel an overwhelming desire to shove her into the firepit. A firm hand squeezes my arm.

"Come," Ayana says and leads me back to the platform. Kai has woken up and is crying. I reach for him and he calms, as does my flame.

"May I share a story?" Ayana asks and the chamber murmurs assent. Ayana sits down and crosses her legs next to me on the platform. Kentaro on my other side snorts. Kai reaches for Ayana and she cuddles him close to her chest and begins.

"A brave hunter had collected every weapon known to his land. The sharpest sword. The strongest bow. But there was one creature feared even more than him... The snake. When bathing in the river, souls would be lost, their bloated floating shells pierced with two tell-tale fang marks.

"The brave hunter met with the snake and said, 'I will protect you. I could chop your head off right now but I won't if you promise never to bite me when I bathe.'

"The snake rose to meet the brave hunter's gaze, liked what she saw, then slithered away. The brave hunter smiled.

"The next day, the brave hunter slid into the river. The water cooled his skin and he closed his eyes to rest.

"There was a ripple and then his eyes clicked open. He raised his foot and saw two bright-red puncture marks near his ankle. The venom spread quickly but he had time to ask, 'Why?'

"'Because I am a snake.'"

The chamber roars with laughter. Ayana makes the shape of a snake with her hand and wriggles it over Kai. He giggles. I glance at Kentaro and see his face is as still as the stone walls. Ayana looks at me and winks. I turn away from Kentaro and join the laughter of my chamber.

There is too much empty space in the temple. Kentaro and I are not enough to fill it. There is a simple solution but Kentaro doesn't understand.

"I feel like I am losing you," Kentaro says, punching the wall in frustration. "Why would you want her here? Am I not enough for you?"

It is not about Kentaro. I want Ayana to live in the temple because it is a hassle to have to wait to see her each rise. Wouldn't it be easier for her and Kai and the rest of her mayus to live here?

"It is what I want," I say.

Kentaro cradles his scraped fist. I don't comfort him. I need to help Ayana move her things from her hut to the temple.

I ratty well shouldn't have bothered moving Ayana into the temple because she is never here. Kentaro mopes around the temple, Haru, Hana, and Riku squeal about and Ayana scuttles out at first light. The only constant is Kai.

I need to hunt. I hang my bow and arrow over my shoulder and enter the jungle.

My jungle is different to Mu. It is warmer here. The

ground and air are moist. There used to be pockets in Mu's jungle that could be almost cool, but here the heat is constant. Roots bulge from the soil, trying to catch a breath above ground. The leaves are wide and flat like bright-green spread palms.

Crack. A twig snaps. Something is here.

I carefully draw an arrow and load my bow, approaching the sound. I hide behind a thick tree trunk and peer around. I would recognise her shadow anywhere. It is Ayana. She is creeping over the roots, clearly not wanting to be seen or heard. I lean against the tree trunk and follow her with my ears. When I am sure she won't realise I am tracking her, I trace her footprints. She becomes easy prey after she treks past the tangle of jungle floor to an area full of mud. The tinkle of water pierces the dense foliage. I hurry to see Ayana's destination and the gurgle of water becomes a roar. Bursting from a crack in a rock face is a huge waterfall.

Ayana unwraps the strip of cloth from her chest then unties the cloth around her waist and puts down her dagger and some other things I can't see that were tucked in her skirt. My shell tingles at the sight of her naked. She is beautiful. Her dark stomach sags from carrying Kai and is covered in silver snail trails, as are her thighs. Between her legs is a full bush of curly black hair. Her nipples, unlike Kentaro's which are small and tight, stick out and are framed by large brown circles.

Her legs and arms I know; I have seen them many times. They are strong and lean but the rest of her looks so soft. I want to touch her and take her flesh between my teeth. Ayana slides into the creek. She wades across to the waterfall and is enveloped in a light mist.

I lie down in the reeds by the water and hold my hardness in my hand. I close my eyes and imagine the softness of Ayana and the firmness of Kentaro and pull until my desire overflows.

When I open my eyes she has gone. I jump up in panic and see she has dressed and is now hurrying along the creek on the opposite bank. I chase her along my bank, being sure to hide in the reeds, and she stops where the creek becomes a river. I crouch low on the riverbank and watch Ayana closely.

She plucks long golden reeds from the grass and begins to weave them. Soon she has woven enough to make what looks like a tiny raft, which is maybe one or two hands long. Ayana raises the raft up to the sky, her mouth muttering words I can't hear. She kisses it and dips it into the water, still muttering, then gently begins smearing handfuls of dark soil over the surface. Her shoulders heave heavily up and down and I realise she is sobbing. Her entire shell shudders. She continues to cry, rests the raft down, and disappears into the trees. I almost stand to see where she has gone but she quickly returns with a red flower. From the band of her skirt she draws a bloodstone and a dagger. She strikes the stone and I have to swallow the urge to help her draw flame. Ayana sparks the stone over the flower's petal and it ignites. She quickly places the flame flower on the raft and gently pushes it downstream.

What the ratty hell?

Maybe I should leave now and get back to our temple before she does. *Is she leaving?* Ayana is sobbing again, as she kneels and places both of her hands in the river. The raft, which was bobbing, seems to change direction and come towards me. I crouch as low as I can but I am startled to hear a rustling near me. I barely breathe. I hear the scrape of a blade against stone and the whisper of fire. *What is going on?* The raft appears again in the middle of the river but now with two flowers burning. It returns with purpose to Ayana's side of the river but a little further along. The reeds tremble and Miki appears with a burning flower. She lays it on the raft, kneels on the soil, wipes tears from her eyes, and it sails again down the river, collecting scorched petals from another broken-hearted she…

What the ratty hell?

"Kentaro?"

"Yes?" Kentaro rolls over, eager to talk. I had been pretending to be asleep.

"Do you know that she called Miki?" I ask.

"The one who told that strange star story?" Kentaro says.

"Yes. Do you remember her from Mu?"

Kentaro looks at me in surprise. "Yes. Are you joking? How can I ever forget? She was with Naho on top of the temple when the unnamed was—"

He doesn't finish the sentence.

I *knew* it. I knew I recognised her from somewhere. It's no wonder that when she's near I can taste death.

"Are you okay?" Kentaro asks, trying to wrap himself around me. I shrug him off.

"Yes," I lie, burning flowers still sailing across my mind.

Kentaro rolls away again and a mound of petal ash rests between us.

NINE

Kairi

May - Orbit Three

The fire pit crackles and Goro and Sana glare at each other across the flames. I don't know why she is here. I thought Matsu was the leader of that tribe. The truth is that until they turn up carrying problems and dump them in my temple, I don't really know what is going on in their villages. I mean, look at Goro! Ratty hell, he looks incredible. He has pierced his ears with various fish bones all along the top down to the lobe. There is also a fish bone shoved through his nose, and he and the others from his tribe, who are standing in front of me now bristling with a rage they haven't yet explained, have painted their scarred forearms and scarred legs blue. What I do know about Goro's tribe is that they settled near a river full of meaty fish that is the envy of the other tribes. All the tribes pay their respects to me with an offering every moon. Goro's is by far the most abundant. His river is second only to my jungle, which is full of tapir, the boar-like beast we discovered when we first landed.

Matsu's tribe, which Sana seems inexplicably to be leading, settled near fields perfect for growing vegetables. Their offering is consistent but it is never as exciting to receive a basket of roots as it is to receive fish or even some of the fruit that the other tribes harvest. Sana has braided her hair exactly as she would have on Mu. The only difference is her croprows are woven through with straw, a golden streak through her dark black hair. She has turned to face me with a defiant stare but the rest of her tribe stand calmly with an expectant look on their faces. They also look like they could have just strolled in from the May side of Mu. They have one lashed arm and the only changes in their appearance are bracelets of straw decorating their wrists and ankles.

Kentaro, Ayana, and I settle on the raised platform and face Goro and Sana. Their tribes fall back a little to listen.

"What happened?" I ask. Sana begins to speak but I hold up my hand to silence her and Goro bows and begins again.

"We have always treated Matsu's tribe with respect," Goro says. I nod, appreciating his refusal to acknowledge

Sana as the new leader. "But they have spat on our trust and behaved without honour."

Sana again makes to speak but I shake my head and she stops. Ayana shifts a little beside me. Goro continues.

"We exchange our fish fairly for their roots"—Sana shakes her head violently and Goro ignores her—"but there was one amongst them who believed they deserved more and they took without barter."

Kentaro and I exchange a glance. For ratty hell's sake, this is the last thing I need right now. It had been going so well. I received my offerings and the tribes bartered between themselves. Simple. One fish for four roots. A tapir for six fish. Everyone was happy.

"They don't barter fairly," Sana shouts. I stare at her. "They were asking for ten roots for one fish! It is too much. Our fields don't flow like their river. We have to harvest and replant. They can fish every rise."

"Why are you here shrieking in my temple?" I ask.

Sana gulps.

"Where is Matsu?"

"He passed," Sana says. "He cut himself harvesting the turnips. The wound never healed and"—she pauses and sighs—"he passed."

"But that doesn't explain why you are here," I say. Sana stares into my face with a hatred I haven't seen since Kaori on Mu. But did Sana honestly believe she was going to walk into my temple as uncontested leader?

None of the pod leaders were a she. So why the ratty hell does Sana think she can take over from Matsu here on May?

"I don't recognise you as the leader of one of my tribes. And you are a carrier. You have your mayu to look after," I say. I have seen her mayu. Kai likes to play with her sometimes in the grass outside of the temple – they are of a similar orbit in age. I have seen them – Sana, Ayana, Kai, and Sana's mayu – Kao, I think her name is.

Sana blinks furiously. "But Matsu chose me. My tribe accept me. I was a rural on Mu. I have the most knowledge about the fields."

"It was not Matsu's decision to make. And clearly you don't have the most knowledge because why can't you produce enough to barter well?"

Sana blinks again and this time tears fall. "I have. I mean, I do. You wouldn't allow this, would you?" she asks and turns to face her tribe. No one meets her eye.

"I need another leader. *Now.*"

Goro smiles, watching Sana gasp like a fish out of water. Her tribe push a he up to my platform.

"Who are you?" I ask.

"My name is Kin," a tall, slim Mayan whispers. "I was also a rural." Kin nods at Kentaro and Kentaro in turn nods his approval at me.

"Okay, Kin. What happened?"

Sana continues to gasp.

Kin looks at her and shrugs reluctantly. Sana searches my face, Kentaro's, and then lands on Ayana. I turn to face Ayana and watch as she almost imperceptibly shakes her head at Sana. Finally, Sana crumples and folds herself back into the pocket of the tribe where she belongs.

"Well … I don't really…" Kin mumbles. Great. They might as well have chosen a root vegetable as leader.

"Goro?" I open the door for him to take over and he sprints through it.

"We found one of them trying to haul a net of fish out of our village. She had to be punished."

She? What the ratty hell is wrong with this vegetable tribe. Why can't they control their shes?

"Where is she?" I ask.

Both tribes rustle.

"I killed her," Goro says without flinching.

Sorry, what? Kentaro and Ayana are united for once – in horror. They both gasp.

Kin nods mutely.

"I slit her throat there and then," Goro explains, seemingly oblivious to the reaction he is provoking.

Sometimes, even though I desperately want to leave him submerged with Mu, I have to think, *what would Takanori do?* He would always choose power. I look from bone-riddled Goro to straw-bracelet-wearing Kin.

"That is an appropriate punishment," I say.

Kentaro grunts in disgust but Ayana keeps her face impassive … except for a twitch in her eyebrow, which betrays her shock, but is only visible to me. Maybe I should send Kentaro to live with Goro to learn what happens when Mayans can't control their impulses. I am so sick of him showing his dissent so openly.

Kin's tribe no longer share a calm, expectant face. They are furious. I know they were expecting the judgement of the Experienced: forbidden to kill, a life for a life. But it is better if they fear each other rather than hate me for intervening.

Kin's tribe are muttering and urging him to say something.

"I … the thing is, they didn't return the shell," Kin says, finally confronting Goro. "You should have returned her."

Goro puffs out his chest. "If she invades *my* village, she belongs to me."

Kentaro pokes me in the side. I don't need it. Goro's words sent a shiver down my spine too and reveal more than he intended.

He will have to be controlled.

But not yet.

Kai wriggles from Kentaro's grasp and runs to join Hana, Riku, and Haru who are playing a game with pebbles on the floor in our sleeping chamber. They have each painted their pebble a different colour and are trying to see who can throw it and land closest to the wall. Ayana is lying across our bed, staring up at the ceiling. We now all sleep together – me, Kentaro, Ayana, and the mayus in the same room on the floor. Kentaro and I barely kiss each other anymore never mind anything else, so there are no problems with us all being together all of the time.

"What are you going to do about Goro?" Ayana asks, still surveying the ceiling.

Kentaro walks over and sits next to Ayana. They both watch me. I glance at the mayus who are squawking over Kai's refusal to stop trying to chew all the pebbles.

I don't know, but I need to do *something*. It has been a moon since his arrogance in my chamber and the thought of it still makes me want to rip the fishbone from his nose and ram it down his throat. Who the ratty hell is he to decide who lives and who dies on my island? And not only that, but also how they enter the eternal? He shouldn't have killed her and he should never have kept the shell.

"What do you think?" I ask, looking at Kentaro and Ayana sitting together. It is a strange sight and indicative of how bad this could be with Goro.

Ayana and Kentaro exchange a glance.

"I think," Kentaro begins, "that you have to do something, and soon, but I have no idea what."

Thanks, Kentaro. Really helpful.

"Do you have any ideas, Ayana?" Kentaro asks.

Even the mayus pause in their squabbles to witness Kentaro inviting Ayana's opinion.

Ayana rubs her temples in gentle circles and sighs. "The Experienced were twelve in number. Even though Takanori was ultimately the leader, it at least seemed that judgement had been passed by *twelve* not one. Of course you cannot allow Goro, or anyone else, to kill without your permission. But I don't think it will be good for you to have the sole responsibility for all those deaths. Because now Goro has killed, it is only a matter of time before the other tribes start killing as punishment too."

Kentaro nods gravely. I also agree. But what can I do?

"So we have to put the responsibility elsewhere. The Experienced also had Namu May Mu – devotion to the island. Their sacrifices were said to restore balance on the island. Now we know Goro killed the she"—Ayana scowls—"because he thought he could. He took without any fear of consequence. But maybe you can tell a new tale of what happened."

I watch Ayana carefully. A new story?

"The she wouldn't have died if there was an abundance of vegetables in their tribe. So she was sacrificed as an offering, her life exchanged for a more fruitful harvest. Did you ever play the gods game when you were an unnamed in the temple?"

Kentaro and I nod. Everyone on Mu played some variant of it.

"We know the gods game!" Hana shouts. "Quick, Haru, come here." Haru rushes over. Hana then says, "The gods say jump up and down."

Immediately Haru starts leaping up and down. Riku runs over to join in.

"The gods say touch your nose," Hana says, and they both touch their nose. "Touch the floor!" Haru stays still but Riku makes to bend down. Hana points and laughs. "Oh no, the gods didn't say so, Riku!"

We all manage to laugh despite the weight of Goro actions.

"Now go back and finish playing pebbles before Kai eats them all!" Ayana says with a smile and they scurry back to retrieve their pebbles from Kai's mouth.

"So let's play the gods game." Ayana smiles a little at the confusion on my face. "The harvest god says a Mayan must be sacrificed to earn a bounty. In the other tribes, the water god demands payment for all the fish or the jungle god for all the beasts. Not Kairi."

No, not me.

"You are just doing the work of the gods. It is not 'Kairi says'. The gods speak *through* you," Kentaro adds, chewing on the idea and clearly enjoying the taste.

It is so simple. Will the Mayans accept this? They were once Maymuans. And Maymuans went to great lengths to defend killing. It is more likely they will seize this justification than choose not to kill each other.

Yes. This could work.

TEN

Kairi

May - Orbit Four

The tribes have assembled at the foot of my pyramid. At the top, on the open platform, I wait, along with Ayana, Kentaro, and the tribe leaders. The leaders twitch, afraid of what they are about to witness. They should be afraid. Above, white clouds swarm and provide fleeting shade from the burning sun.

There is commotion below as those assembled begin to part and a blue shell is escorted by my pack and five other Mayans up the stairs of the pyramid. I admire Goro for not resisting. I rise to greet him as he ascends and approaches his death. His fishbones are gone and he wears only a loincloth. His entire shell has been dyed blue with crushed indigo leaves. He is the colour of the river in which his fish swim. He stares at me. I bow to him but he sneers.

"Well done, Kairi," Goro croaks, his blue throat dry. He licks his cracked lips and looks at the basket of iridescent fish sitting on an elevated plinth. "Even I, who have studied your cruelty, never expected this."

I can't take full credit. Beside me, Ayana glistens in a gold ceremonial dress encrusted with blue beading.

"Lie down," Ayana barks and points to the flat stone table in the centre of the platform.

Goro shows his first sign of resistance. He bares his teeth at Ayana. Each tooth has been filed into a crocodile-sharp point.

Ayana leans in to his face and snarls, "Lay him down."

The Mayans who escorted Goro up the pyramid push him towards the ceremonial table. Goro takes a final deep breath and lies down, facing the sun, his back flat on the stone. The pack hold him down, Ikki and Shun wrapping their fists tightly around his ankles. Tetsu and another Mayan hold his wrists so he is spread like a bird for slaughter.

Ayana approaches a smaller table next to Goro and unwraps a piece of black cloth. Inside, various sharpened bones glisten. She inspects a long, thin stingray spine, appropriate for a he of the sea, and after piercing her own fingertip to check the spike, she turns to Goro.

Goro's chest heaves up and down and sweat smears the blue dye on his brow. His head swivels as he searches for something.

"Not her. Kairi! Kairi, you do it. I don't want to leave this time by the hand of a she."

Ayana and I lock eyes. I am surprised. I thought Goro was going to make a final plea for his life. I will not give him what he has asked for. It is not a she. It is Ayana.

The moment passes and Ayana continues with the sacrifice. The Mayan holding his right arm pushes down hard on his hand and elbow until Goro's veins bulge beneath his blue skin. Ayana slowly inserts the stingray spine through his wrist until it pierces the other side and scratches the stone table. Blood pools and the Mayans not holding Goro dip their palms and smear the blood on the fish in the basket on the plinth. The fish turn red and I thank the imaginary gods for delivering the perfect way to end Goro.

The catch from his ratty river had finally dwindled. When the tribe delivered their once-a-moon basket and it had fewer fish than usual, I was excited. The next two moons they delivered even fewer and I knew Goro was finished.

Goro moans now as Ayana inserts the stingray spine into his other wrist, held by Tetsu. More of his blood drains and I hear a retching sound behind me. Kentaro and I turn to see Kin sweating and vomiting. The other tribe leaders don't look too well either.

I turn back and see Tetsu has let go of Goro's pierced wrist.

"Be careful," I shout, but before the words even touch the air Goro has swivelled and sunk his teeth into Ayana's arm.

Blood spurts and Ayana screams.

"Hold him! Don't let him go!" I shout. Kentaro seizes Goro's jaw and yanks it apart to release Ayana's arm.

There is a dull thud behind me and I don't even need to look to know Kin has fainted. Kentaro pulls the cloth from underneath the sharpened bones and they land with a clatter on the floor. He wraps the cloth around Ayana's wound. Goro writhes and gurgles a mouthful of Ayana's blood. Ikki and Shun gain control of his legs and two other Mayans wrestle his wrists until he is back in the sacrificial position.

I lunge at Tetsu and he backs away until he is teetering on the top of the pyramid staircase.

"You're next," I hiss.

Tetsu's eyes widen and he gulps. Then he closes his eyes and seems to make a decision. He leans back.

The crack of his skull against the stone stairs rings through the air. Again and again.

I feel as sick as Kin.

"Don't let him go!" I hear someone scream. I turn and

see again that Goro is almost free. Ayana is shouting at Ikki and Shun, who are blinking as if to erase the image of Tetsu falling.

"Kairi, we have to finish this," Ayana yells. She holds out her wrapped arm to Kentaro. "Tie that tight!"

With the bandage now secure, Ayana takes control.

Goro's ankles are pierced with the stingray spine and so much blood is poured into the offering basket that the fish look like skinned tapir. Soon Goro is too drained to even moan. Which, considering what will happen to him next, is merciful.

Kentaro picks up a large, cruel-looking sharpened bone and hands it to Ayana. She positions the point beneath Goro's chin and leans heavily on it, using all of her weight to force the blade deep into his shell. She carves in a straight line to his belly button. The tribe leaders cry out as if it is their chests being desecrated.

I will have my role to play soon in this sacrifice, but watching Ayana elbow-deep inside Goro's shell is making my stomach churn. She inserts both hands and spreads Goro's ribs. The crack silences the tribe leaders. They cover their mouths with their hands. Kin, now awake, sobs into his.

I approach the shell. I peer into Goro's open chest and locate his still beating heart.

I take my bloodstone and strike my dagger against it

until it sparks. Heat surges across my shoulders and down my arm.

I flick my finger and Goro's heart is set aflame.

It is too much. For everyone.

Ikki and Shun run from what is left of Goro and huddle together with the tribe leaders. Kentaro, Ayana, and I stare into the fire.

I don't know about appeased gods but I see devils dancing in the cavity.

ELEVEN

Kairi

May - Orbit Seven

"Kairi? Sana is here to see you," Ayana says with a smile. "Sorry to interrupt such a beautiful rise."

Sunlight shines through the slits high in the temple wall. Kentaro, the mayus, and I are lying in our chamber. I suppose they are not mayus anymore. Tucked under my arm is Hana – she is eleven orbits. Riku, who is now fifteen orbits, and Haru, who is thirteen, no longer share our chamber – they have their own huts outside the temple. Riku and Haru have become such exceptional hunters they have joined my pack. Together with Ikki and Shun, they provide a constant supply of tapir and are instrumental in the once-a-moon sacrificial ceremony.

Kai is seven orbits old and his long shell is curled around Kentaro. I try and impress Kai with my roaring flames or by placing a fruit on the other side of the room and piercing it with an arrow from my bow, but he would rather sit in silence watching Kentaro weave a basket. Kai is infatuated with him. Kentaro feigns indifference but when Kai hurries to claim the space next to him, Kentaro can't control the flush of his cheeks and the sparkle in his eye.

I gently extract my arm from under Hana's head and stand up. I wonder what Sana wants? I hope they have chosen an acceptable new leader. Kin had a good reign. His tribe met their offering quota for almost three orbits. I thought I was never going to get rid of him. Not that I particularly wanted to, but all of the other tribes had experienced their leaders being sacrificed at least once. It was becoming noticeable that Kin was the only constant at the leaders' meetings. Finally a downpour of rain drowned their crop, rotting the roots. Their reserves only lasted for one more offering before they had to concede defeat.

Surely Sana is not reckless enough to have entered my temple to confront me about Kin's sacrifice? It was ... unfortunate. I shiver. I exit my chamber and climb the stairs to the meeting chamber.

The previous night's embers smoulder in the fire pit and the chamber smells of smoke. Sana is standing with her back to me and with her mayu, Kao, at her side. They stare into the charred remains. I place my hand on

Sana's shoulder and she spins around in fear. I stare at her and she swiftly regains composure. She reminds me of Ayana and how quickly she can fix her face from one extreme emotion to another in a blink. Maybe it is a she thing? Kao peers up at me. She doesn't really look like Sana but her face is familiar. She has had the same growth spurt as Kai – her legs seem as unstable as a fawn's.

"What do you want?" I ask.

Sana takes a deep breath. "I want to be the new leader."

I roll my eyes and walk way. Not this again. Sana grabs my shoulder and spins me around.

"Don't you ever touch me," I hiss at her.

Kao gasps but Sana stands her ground. *Who does this she think she is?*

I lean towards Sana. "I told you last time. I will *never* allow a she to lead."

Sana chews her bottom lip. "Have the tribe from the cove presented their new leader yet?"

My eyes narrow. How does she know about that? Ratty shell-picking weaklings. No, they haven't, and neither have the tribe from the other side of the jungle who offer fruit.

"You will be waiting a while," Sana says then, a smile playing around her lips.

I hate this she.

"Why?" a voice from behind me asks, and I turn, startled.

"Hello, Ayana," Sana says with a bow.

"Sana," Ayana replies with a nod of her head.

I look from Sana to Ayana and feel a panic I can't remove from my face. Ayana stands beside me and runs her hand over my shaved head and strokes my back until I feel almost calm.

Kao stares at Ayana until she garners her attention. Ayana smiles. "Would you like to see Kai?"

Kao nods.

Ayana points to the door she just came through, which is still slightly ajar. Kao skips happily away from us and closes the door.

"Why haven't the cove presented a new leader?" Ayana asks.

"They are too afraid," Sana says. "After Kin's sacrifice no one wants to be leader. Even before then there was hesitation but now … no one wants to do it."

Ayana sighs and shakes her head. I could punch the fire pit in frustration. The embers crackle and spit in rhythm with my thumping heart.

"Ratty Kin," I mutter.

"You can't blame Kin for what happened!" Sana snaps.

I am going to kill this she.

"I think what Sana means," Ayana says with a

pointed look at Sana, "is that the previous rebellions didn't help."

"Ratty Tetsu then," I say, instantly regretting my whining tone. I need to regain control. I can't lose it in front of this she, Sana. But this conversation is really making my stomach churn. After Tetsu launched himself down the temple staircase, breaking every bone in his shell during Goro's sacrifice, some of the following sacrifices have tried to do the same.

Instead of lying on the altar and accepting their fate, they clamber off the table and make a run for the staircase. It was an impossible situation, because when Riku and Haru first joined the pack they were unable to restrain the unwilling sacrifice. Shun and Ikki couldn't hold the leader and protect me, Ayana, and Kentaro at the same time, so we lost four leaders to the staircase.

With Kin, no one expected him to have the pride to try and take his own life, so the pack were barely holding him. I care deeply about Riku, Haru, and Hana. I still favour Kai as the first born of May, but the truth is I love them all. So I didn't want to punish Riku and Haru for letting go of previous leaders, but I had to do something. I told them, Ikki and Shun too, that under no circumstance could another sacrifice escape to take their own life and end up as a pile of shattered bones in a flesh bag at the bottom of the staircase in front of all the other Mayans. It could not happen again.

When Ayana inserted the stingray spine into Kin's wrist, he leapt up as if struck by lightning. Riku and Haru each grabbed a sharpened bone each from Ayana's kit and began stabbing Kin in a frenzied attack. He ended up in no fit state to be sacrificed. Ayana performed the only merciful act available and pierced his heart with the stingray spine. Everywhere, except the sacrificial basket of roots, was covered in his blood.

Since then, we have had to subdue the sacrifices. Kentaro recognised a tree similar to one on Mu. We call it kaka. The roots of this tree can be used to make a powerful draught that numbs the limbs but not the mind. A stronger draught could easily stop a heart, but we have continued with live, but immobile, sacrifices.

Ayana looks to me. "What has Sana asked?"

"I want—" Sana begins but Ayana mutes her with a glare.

"What does she want?" Ayana asks again, as if Sana is not there.

"She still wants to be leader. I told her it is impossible."

"Why?" Ayana asks.

"*Why?*" I scoff. "You know why. There has never been a she leader. Not in the pods or in the tribes." I look at Sana who is listening intently but thankfully silently. I would rather not talk about this in front of her. She doesn't deserve an explanation but Ayana is ploughing on regardless.

"If the hes are too afraid then the leaders will have to be shes." Ayana says this as if it is that simple, but I cannot have a swarm of cockroach Kaoris ruling my villages. "Some of the Experienced were shes," Ayana adds.

"I do not want to talk about Mu," I hiss. "This is not Mu."

"Okay. But, Kairi, consider this. Does it really matter if the leaders are he or she if they will all be sacrificed within one or two orbits?"

I can't believe she just said that in front of Sana. Look at Sana! She is nodding in agreement. What the ratty hell is wrong with her? She is instigating her own destruction.

Ayana and Sana look at me expectantly.

"I will think about it," I say.

The last of the embers in the fire no longer glow.

"I have been thinking about your death," Ayana says.

I drop the leg of tapir I was eating. Kentaro chokes a little on the meat he was chewing.

"If you died, what would happen?" Ayana muses.

"What do you mean what would happen?" Kentaro

splutters. "Why are you even thinking about Kairi dying?"

Ayana pushes scraps of meat around her woven plate with her finger. "I was just thinking … if you died, would Kentaro lead? Would the tribes even accept him as leader?"

"I don't want to lead," Kentaro says, indignant at the thought.

Good, because I don't think they would accept him as leader.

"I don't want Kairi to die," Hana says, her voice trembling.

Ayana rushes over to cuddle her. "Kairi is not dying. Don't worry."

"Then why did you say it?" Hana asks, holding Ayana tight.

"We will all return to the eternal eventually, and because Kairi has great responsibility we must be prepared."

"I don't like it." Hana shakes her head violently from side to side.

Kai begins to squirm in his seat. "Ken-kun I don't like it." Tears shine in his eyes and his chin trembles.

"Come here," Kentaro says and Kai leaps up and dives into Kentaro's arms.

"What are you thinking?" I ask Ayana, trying to ignore the distressed mayus.

"Do we really have to discuss this now?" Kentaro says, looking from troubled Hana to trembling Kai.

"Hana," Ayana says, "take Kai to our chamber and wait for us in there."

"I don't want to."

"Now," Ayana says and gives Hana a gentle push. Hana walks over to collect Kai. He agrees to leave after an extra squeeze from Kentaro.

I watch Hana lead Kai out of our eating chamber. The door closes softly behind them.

"Do you care about us?" Ayana asks.

Where are these strange questions coming from?

"Yes," I say.

"Then you must put something in place in case we ever have to go on without you," Ayana says.

"If Kairi died then I would die too," Kentaro says without hesitation.

Ayana raises an eyebrow. "Well, I am sure your loyalty is sincere, but what about Kai? Would you leave him here? In this time? Alone?"

Kentaro flinches as if she has struck him.

"No," I say, "you wouldn't." Kentaro looks torn. "It's okay. She's right. You must protect the mayus. All of them. We have to consider beyond now."

But what can I do?

"If not Kentaro as leader, then how would you feel about Kai?" Ayana says.

Kai? I thought she was going to suggest herself. So did Kentaro by the expression on his face.

Kai?

"But he is only seven orbits," I say.

"No one is expecting you to die right now, Kairi! But if you did we would be here to help Kai. Wouldn't we?" Ayana says to Kentaro.

Kentaro is still in shock from the whole conversation. He nods dumbly.

"So what are you suggesting? That I start telling everyone Kai is to replace me? Won't that seem a bit strange?" I say.

"Yes, it would. I don't think you should talk of him replacing you. I think you should declare him your heir. You know, like the jungle cats do. They have a dominant leader and when they die their status is transferred to their heir. Their mayu."

"But everyone here knows Kai is not Kairi's mayu! They might not literally remember Reo"—I glare at Kentaro for mentioning that name and Ayana's fist clenches—"but they know Kairi did not create him."

The unexpected mention of Reo has rattled Ayana more than I have ever witnessed. She stares blindly at the door.

"Ayana?" I say, and touch her shoulder. She reaches up and covers my hand with hers. Her nails dig into my skin. "Ayana?"

Her grip softens and she lays her palm on my hand.

"We will have to combine your blood. It is the only way."

Kentaro and I look at each other. I hear the crack of Goro's ribs and the sizzle of his heart.

Kentaro stands up and leers over Ayana. "You cannot cut Kai on your ratty sacrificial table! Or Kairi."

"I have to," Ayana says.

"You are not going to butcher them like the other leaders! Find another way," Kentaro shouts.

"We have to respect the gods," Ayana says. Kentaro snorts but she continues, "It must be an offering of blood."

"You do remember we made up the gods, don't you?' Kentaro says.

"All right, Kentaro, that's enough," I say.

"But, Kairi—"

"No," I say. "It will be blood. For the gods."

I stare at him and dare him to say that the gods don't exist again. Kentaro swallows his anger and remains silent. But it will be blood from a place that heals well and can be soothed quickly.

I am at the foot of my pyramid surrounded by ecstatic Mayans. Unlike the sacrifices, Kai and I are not painted blue but we are surrounded by my pack. Kai is trembling. I hold his hand firmly in mine but he flinches every time an overeager Mayan reaches out to touch him. Riku and Haru try and swat them away, but there are too many. One rise, these will be his Mayans so he will have to learn not only to embrace their adulation but also to control it.

We ascend the stone staircase. Waiting to greet us at the top are Ayana and Kentaro. I feel Kai lurch forward to embrace them but I hold him tight. I told him repeatedly that we are outside the temple not within. We do not wear the same mask outside as we do inside. I squish Kai's hand in mine and he bows his head in regret.

Kentaro looks like he is about to forget where he is too. I can see he is desperate to comfort Kai. I hand Kai directly to Ayana, who leads him to the ceremonial altar with an indifference that makes it hard to believe she was his carrier. The pack prepare to hold him down but Kentaro yelps and shoos Ikki and Shun away. They look relieved. Haru and Riku gently hold Kai's legs and Kentaro leans over and strokes Kai's hair. Kai's frantic chest stops pumping and he calms and lets Kentaro hold his wrists above his head.

Ayana hovers over her sacrificial kit. I look at the assembled leaders watching the ceremony. The newly appointed leader from the cove nods in greeting to me. I return her respect. Sana also tries to catch my eye but I ignore her. Ratty know-it-all Sana.

The glint of the stingray spine in the midday sun returns my attention to the ceremony. Ayana leans over Kai, and Kentaro sweats, watching her like a Maymuan nabgar. Ayana's mouth mumbles words for only Kai to hear. She is facing towards me so I can lip read. "Don't be afraid, my love. I would never hurt you."

Kai reluctantly sticks his tongue out. Ayana swiftly pierces the spine through it and Kai is done. I am sure he has a mouthful of blood but he will be okay. Ayana smears Kai's blood across a bundle of white cloth in the offering basket.

Kentaro leads Kai from the altar and gives him a cup of sea water to gargle and spit.

The pack look to me. Ikki and Shun clearly do not want to hold me down. Haru and Riku just look excited.

I dismiss them with a flick of my wrist and they stand back from the altar. I lie down and gaze into the sky. Strong winds have painted long strips of cloud across the blue. In their undulation I see a snake.

Kaori.

My tongue becomes heavy in my mouth as my mind replays Kaori piercing the venom gland of the snake she caught when I was her torchbearer, how she smeared the poison across her tongue and then mine. I could barely speak but she had ingested so much venom during her hunts that she seemed immune. Like all the water hunters.

Ayana's face is above mine now. I sit up so fast we almost knock foreheads. Ayana looks from me to the staircase in confusion. No. I am not about to dive down there, but I am not letting you stick anything in my mouth. I snatch the stingray spine and pierce my own tongue. Blood spurts but I drink it down and quickly smear the spine across the cloth already stained by Kai.

Ayana remains open-mouthed until Riku nudges her.

"Mayan gods of land, sea, and air," Ayana bellows, "we present to you May's honourable heir."

The assembled leaders cheer and I beckon Kai. We stand at the top of the staircase. The Mayans below roar their approval. Kai smiles, his tongue still tender. I retch a little from the overwhelming amount of blood pooling in my mouth. Riku passes me a bloodstone and a dagger. I make a spark and although I feel dizzy, I manage to ignite the offering basket and our prayer for an heir is delivered to the gods.

TWELVE

Kairi

May – Orbit Eight

Rays of sunlight pierce the gaps between the heavy leaves and vines of May jungle. I squat into the sludge. Eyes on my prey. A tapir snuffles the dirt, unaware that Riku, Haru, and I have it surrounded. I exhale a piercing whistle and we strike.

Riku shoots an arrow which lands perfectly into the beast's neck. It slumps to the ground and Haru throws a net woven from vines over its thrashing legs. We leer over the tapir watching the blood seep from its neck. Riku pulls out his arrow, inserts a blade and slits the tapir's throat for a swift slaughter.

"Excellent Riku." I say, impressed, "And Kentaro has taught you well too, Haru." I run my hand over the net that Kentaro has taught Haru to weave.

"On Mu we had to carry the boars without nets."

Riku and Haru exchange an alarmed glance. I laugh, "Don't worry that will not be part of your training. It is much easier to carry the carcass back to the temple in the nets."

We have killed three tapirs today. Without Shun and Ikki. It is clear Riku and Haru are more than capable to replace them.

"Let's refresh a little before we take these back," I say.

Haru swiftly knots the net around the tapir carcass and Riku scales a nearby tree and returns with three green coco.

"I can't believe you would drag the boars without nets," Riku says handing me a coco. I crack it on a rock and gulp the sweet juice from within.

"There are so many things we did on Mu I wouldn't do now," I reply.

"Like what?" Haru asks, unable to hide his enthusiasm about talking about Mu.

I pause in scraping my teeth against the pulp. I have been thinking about Mu a lot lately. And thinking about Takanori. Haru stares at me expectantly, eager for any thoughts about Mu. He has Ayana's nose and her long eyelashes. Riku has her beautiful hair and piercing stare. I love them both. Not how I love and desire Kentaro and Ayana. A different love. I want to protect them. Train them to protect themselves. This love makes thoughts of Takanori intolerable.

How could he have created me with Naho and then make me do all the terrible things on Mu? It was not love. I know this deep within my shell, but still the longing for him remains. One more chance to make everything right. For him to tell me he loved me, too. A dream as elusive as returning to Mu and resurrecting her from the depths.

"Take these back to the temple." I bark. Riku and Haru scramble to their feet and toss their cocos into the trees. My heart throbs at the earnestness of their actions. Their desperation to please me. It is clear they would never betray me. Riku and Haru are all I need.

"Are you sure, Kairi?" Ayana asks, unable to hide her surprise. Kentaro beside her frowns.

"Yes." I say, "I will tell them now."

Ayana and Kentaro follow me into the chamber where Ikki, Shun, and all the mayu are waiting for us to eat supper. In the centre of the table is a whole roasted tapir resting on a plate filled with colourful fruit and vegetables.

"Let's eat." I say, taking my seat. Ayana begins to carve the meat.

Ikki and Shun exchange a nervous glance. Ikki clears his throat and asks, "Did we miss a hunt today?"

"No." I say, accepting a plate of meat from Ayana.

"We caught this one." Haru says happily.

Hana claps her hands together in applause and Kai joins in.

Shun shifts uncomfortably in his chair and mumbles thanks to Ayana when she passes him a plateful of food.

Ikki stares at me. Time has not healed his face. It is as ruined as now as it was when I threw the jellyfish at him after Naho's death on Mu.

"You caught a tapir with only three hunters?" Ikki asks incredulously.

"Yes." I reply.

"We caught three and brought them back to the temple." Haru says.

"Enough pride." Ayana snaps and Haru blushes.

"They should be proud. They are both exceptional hunters," I say. Riku and Haru glow with joy.

Ikki sucks his teeth and Kentaro sighs, "Just get it over and done with."

The chair Shun was sat in scrapes across the floor. He is on his feet ready to fight.

"Do you really think you could defeat me in my own temple?" I ask, amused.

Shun doesn't know what to do. His head swivels from furious Ikki to impatient Kentaro.

"They don't deserve this." Kentaro says.

Ikki and Shun step closer together. Ikki's eyes are blazing more than any fire I have ever sparked.

"You have served me well," I say looking from Ikki to Shun, "But I don't need you anymore."

They brace themselves, unsure from whom the blow will strike.

"You can go."

Ikki blinks rapidly in surprise and Shun clutches Ikki's arm.

"Go?" Ikki repeats.

"Yes," I say, "Choose a tribe and go."

Wonder spreads across their faces as their freedom dawns.

They begin to back away towards the door. Ayana smiles. Hana and Kai wave. Ecstatic, they turn and sprint with indecent haste out of my temple without so much as a thank you. Good riddance. I have all I ever need with me here in this room now.

"They don't deserve this," [illegible]

[illegible] than another. There even smiled [illegible]

"You have saved everyone," I say, looking from [illegible] to [illegible]. "[illegible] you anyway."

[illegible] themselves, [illegible] whom [illegible]. They will smile.

[illegible]

[illegible] and [illegible] clutches [illegible]

[illegible] repeats.

[illegible] Choose a [illegible] and go.

[illegible] wonder spreads across [illegible] faces as they [illegible]

They begin to back away towards the door. [illegible] they turn and [illegible] without [illegible] a [illegible] we all [illegible] with [illegible] now.

THIRTEEN

Kairi

May – Orbit Nine

Where is she? My foot taps against the floor and I peer out of the ground floor opening into the forest surrounding the temple.

"We can just go," Kentaro says, impatient to show me what he has discovered. Finally the main door creaks open and Ayana hurries in pushing Hana.

"Where have you been?" I shout. Ayana ignores me and shoves Hana in the direction of the stairs leading to the chamber above.

"I'm sorry," Ayana murmurs, "Has something happened?"

"I asked you where you have been. You are constantly scurrying off somewhere. What the ratty hell are you doing?"

Ayana frowns, "Why are you so upset? Just tell me what has happened."

I inhale ready to exhale a blast of anger at Ayana, but Kentaro interrupts, "We need to go. Now."

Ayana and I follow Kentaro outside into the forest and it quickly becomes clear he is leading us to a river. I stare at Ayana and she shows no recognition that she has been here before. I know she has. It is the river where I saw her and Miki burning flowers. I gasp when we reach the banks.

The river no longer flows, instead a stream trickles. The vast water is no more. I can step through the reeds swaying on the bank and stand on the exposed earth below.

Kentaro traces a finger along the dry cracks of the river bed, "This is why the offerings from all tribes have dwindled."

For the past few moons I have had to accept fewer offerings from all the tribes. It seemed to happen at the same time. One moon they all delivered significantly less. I couldn't sacrifice them all so Ayana and I decided to allow it in the hope that whatever was diminishing the offerings would pass.

Ayana seems lost in the cracks of the riverbed.

"Ayana?" I ask, her head swivels to face mine and I notice how exhausted she looks. Her skin seems as dehydrated as the river bed, "What do you think?"

"I don't know," Ayana sighs, "I am not a rural. I could speak to Sana and ask her what she thinks."

I groan. Ratty know it all Sana, but her tribe is made up of primarily rurals from Mu.

"Okay, ask her. But be sure to remind her if this is not fixed soon, then her and all the other she leaders will be up for sacrifice."

Ayana nods and I am alarmed to see what looks like fear in her eyes. Ayana rushes off to find Sana and I approach Kentaro who is kneeling on the dry riverbed beside the remaining trickle.

"How bad is it Ken-kun?" I ask.

Kentaro shakes his head gravely, "I will need to check the other rivers. If they are like this we will be in serious trouble."

"Why?" I demand.

Kentaro looks at me like I have sprouted another head, "Because we cannot survive without water."

In the gurgle of the stream I hear my twin Kaori laugh at our plight.

"I [illegible]," Aventurine says. "I am not a mortal. I could speak to Sana and ask her what she thinks."

[illegible] Sana, but [illegible] of [illegible] from [illegible]

"Ok," I ask her. "If the [illegible] not [illegible] and soon [illegible] of [illegible] up for sacrifice."

[illegible] in her [illegible] and I [illegible] on the [illegible] beside the remaining [illegible]

"How [illegible]?" I ask.

[illegible] the other [illegible]. If they [illegible] like this [illegible] will be in serious trouble."

"Why?" I demand.

[illegible] head. "Because we cannot [illegible]"

In the [illegible] at [illegible] pitch.

FOURTEEN

Kairi

May – Orbit Ten

Again I look into the cloudless sky and offer up a prayer.

Air gods, I demand you release the moisture from your clouds. Water gods, refill the parched river basin. Namu ratty May Mu. Someone please send water.

The image of Kaori, illuminated by a crack of lightning and drenched in purple rain on my beach after Naho's death, flashes through my mind.

I rub the bloodstone in my palm.

Kaori, can you hear me? I need you. I need water.

I peer down the outer pyramid staircase. Mayans arc gathered at the foot of the pyramid, moaning and crying. They gather every rise but what can I do? It has been over six moons without rain. Even the clouds have deserted us, leaving no filter for the relentless sun. The soil is cracked; fish have no river to swim in; crops are dry and brittle. Goro's third replacement was sacrificed and still the river did not flow. Sana was sacrificed and the roots remained thirsty underground.

"Have they gathered down there again?" Ayana asks, emerging from the inner staircase that leads out of the main chamber onto the sacrificial space. I can hear the murmur of the leaders assembled around the fire pit in the chamber below. I can't listen to them wail any longer. I came up here for calm but I don't feel any better here either. Ayana drapes a cloth over her head to shield her skin from the burning sun. She looks terrible. We are all suffering the effects of only being able to drink the vapour of boiled sea water and eating rations as if we have returned to the ratty pods, but Ayana looks particularly drained. Her skin no longer shines and is a dull brown. Her hair hangs limp. It looks like more than starvation, which is bad enough; it is as if something has stolen all of the energy of her soul from her shell. Whatever made her shine from within has gone.

"Yes. Mymig them! What do they want? For ratty hell's sake, they can see the rain has yet to fall. What can I do?"

Ayana sighs and draws her veil tightly around her neck.

"And what are they saying?" I snap, pointing to the

inner staircase leading to the leaders' meeting. "Do they have any suggestions of how to resolve this? I can't drink one more mouthful of ocean dregs. We shouldn't have used the last of the river watering the grain."

"If we hadn't then we would be in even more trouble than we are now," Ayana says wearily. "Without the grain to grind by the next orbit, there could be nothing left to eat."

I kick a stray loose stone and it rattles down the side of the pyramid. "And what about them?" I ask again.

"The leaders are saying the sacrifices are not working," Ayana says.

"Of course they are! They just don't want to be sacrificed." The sun burns my shoulders but there is no shade to step under.

"They are not the only ones who believe tribe leader sacrifices are not enough," Ayana says. I look at her and see she is watching me carefully.

What the ratty hell does that mean?

"What? You mean those ungrateful rats down there?" I say. "Are we taking guidance from any Mayan now? You got your *she* leaders. Should I just let anyone into my temple now to decide our fate?"

"Kairi, this is serious."

"I know it is serious!" I scream. "What is suggesting to you that I am not taking this ratty seriously?"

Ayana's voice is hoarse and raspy from the drought.

She tries to swallow but I know the feeling when there isn't even enough saliva to soothe the throat. "They are afraid. And panicking. They believe the gods are punishing us. And we have not done enough to appease them." Ayana scowls. "Maybe the gods *are* punishing us."

Don't say Ayana has completely lost her mind now. That is the absolute last thing I need. Her going all Tetsu on me.

I grab her by her shoulders. "You do remember who the gods are, don't you?"

"But maybe because we have made offerings to them, they have really come," Ayana says, her eyes shining with a mania that sours my empty stomach.

There is a scuffle on the inner staircase and Riku and Haru appear, both desperate to tell me something.

Haru catches his breath first and says one word – one word which chills my spine.

"Kentaro."

I rush past them and descend the stairs.

The main chamber is in chaos.

The leaders, now comprised of mainly shes, have seized hold of Kentaro from the main platform and are dragging him towards the fire. Kai, his eyes scrunched tightly closed with effort, is clinging to Kentaro's legs, and his extra weight is the only reason Kentaro has not been consumed by the flames.

A rage so virulent that it actually cools my blood rather than boils trembles through my shell.

I flick my wrist and the fire gasps and retracts. The sudden loss of heat and light shocks the leaders and they release Kentaro. Both he and Kai scramble to their feet and run to my side.

"Get out of my temple," I hiss.

The leaders stare, dumbfounded.

"Get out!" I yell, and my fire erupts, forcing the leaders to flee out of the door.

One.

Furious fists pound the temple doors below. Their anger ricochets across the vast space. Above, footsteps stomp across the roof, searching for their prey. For me.

Two.

Anxious eyes exchange futile glances. Ayana and the mayu, so brave, but it is time. My time.

I must flee, but I have to make sure the others are safe.

Tears spill from Riku, Haru, Hana, and Kai. My mayus. Ayana drags them to safety.

Three.

Kentaro, my love. We can never truly part. You are always my true half. My completion. My whole. Protect the mayus. You can. And you must. Don't let them take Kai.

Four.

They are here.

I lie prone in my own prison – a locked chamber hidden in the base of my temple built to prepare the leaders for sacrifice. Slits high above stream a little sunlight, enough to illuminate the blue sacrificial powder that stains the floor.

I could be swimming. Immersed in cool blue water. Cleansed. Thirsty.

My lips brush the water below. Blue dirt stains my mouth. I cough and splutter, further ravaging my parched throat. It hurts less if I roll and stare at the ceiling.

Sunlight shimmers iridescent dust. I reach out to touch it but barely have the energy to raise my arm. The last of my spirit left trying to fight them. They were too many. And their limbs were fuelled by the zealotry of their conviction. My sacrifice will end the drought. To appease the gods I created, my flesh must be offered. The ultimate sacrifice. But who will perform the ceremony?

The door creaks.

I make to sit up but warm hands push me gently back

down. The door closes and rattles a little as a lock is slid back across.

"I brought you this." A cup is thrust into my hand.

I sip. There is liquid inside. It is terribly bitter but it is wet so I drink it all.

"You can leave me now, Miki," Ayana says and footsteps retreat from the door.

I feel it in my fingers first. A tingling. Not the rumble of flame. Energy. Life. But a numbness too. An emptying. Death.

"Ayana?" I mumble.

"Shush. Just accept it," Ayana hisses. "Believe me, Kairi, you will be grateful to feel nothing." She strokes my forehead and a chill unrelated to the kaka draught she has given me rushes through my spine.

"You will lie here before your death. And you will listen."

My veins flood with the cold of deep sea water.

FIFTEEN

Ayana

May - Orbit Ten

Kairi's fingers twitch in the sliver of sunlight penetrating the gloomy chamber. The paralysing root tea stills the limbs, numbs the senses, but does not close the eyes or ears.

Ayana is surprised to feel pity. He never suspected. Even now his eyes flicker from dilated shock to an expression of pain so fierce it almost makes Ayana regret her betrayal.

Almost.

Ayana walks slowly around Kairi's shell, her footsteps branding the blue floor.

His eyes follow her pace.

"You never freed us," Ayana says, intent on telling Kairi all he has not known before the end, but her tone is as if she is speaking to herself. It is as much her opportunity to document and compile all she has achieved as it is an opportunity to reveal the flaw of Kairi's arrogance. "The carriers were rebelling long before your volcano ripped apart Mu." Ayana pauses and looks down at Kairi. "You never asked. For all the time we shared, for all we have spoken of, did you ever stop to think why I hated the rearers so much?"

No, he hadn't. No one on Mu gave much thought to what the carriers experienced when they disappeared into the forest to fulfil their island duty. There were stories. There are always stories. Of troubled carriers who returned to Mu after creating four or five maymu. Who couldn't reintegrate. Who eventually disappeared again. It was assumed they returned to help the rearers, so enamoured with creating that they couldn't resist the scene of delivery. But the ropes hanging forlorn from the trees past the cob field told another story. Unheard. Lost on the breeze that swayed the stalks and swept away the anguish. No one cared enough to listen to those truths.

A grim smile flashes across Ayana's tired face. "They made sure to avoid your island. After the split. With so many carriers on May, the rearers couldn't dare choose your side. They had to stay on Mu."

Kaori had sailed across the scorched sea with a pod full of rearers and Experienced. Kairi had arrived on the new land with a pod particularly full of carriers.

But it was as if the carriers were rallying around a new leader.

Never Kairi.

Ayana.

"You were surrounded by carriers, in the womb you and Kentaro built to survive the wave," Ayana's mouth fills with a bitterness that curdles her lip. "You are possessed by May. The urge to take and consume. Eyes so fixed on the horizon you can't see what or who is right beside you. How could you be so blind? Goro wanted to be like you – riddled with May. He slit Emi's throat. That's right," Ayana spits, stroking the teeth mark scars Goro had left on her arm during his sacrifice. "Her name was Emi. She had two mayu she needed to feed. She loved her tribe and would do anything for them. Goro slaughtered her like she was a Mu boar. Because of you. Because he wanted to be like you. After I convinced you to sacrifice him, I knew there was only one way this would end. Eventually we would have to sacrifice our most valuable Mayan to appease the gods… You."

Mu loved whispers.

They changed their name but Mayans are and will always be Maymuans. Renegade carriers loyal to Ayana were able to mutter softly into eager Mayan ears: *the tribe leaders are not enough for the gods; the rain will not fall until the blood of the greatest amongst us is spilled.* The carriers whispered with disdain for Kairi in their heart, but it was the respect of his Mayans that sealed his fate. Thoughts of Kairi's sacrifice flowed easily, unlike the barren river. The one we worship must die to save us all. A zealotry worthy of Takanori infected Kairi's acolytes as heady and intoxicating as hunmir smoke.

A crow caws outside the slit and pecks at the stone, obscuring the light and casting frantic flickers of shadow over Ayana's face. "I know what you did to Reo."

Ayana crouches down beside Kairi and leans over him so their eyes are level. Kairi blinks rapidly but cannot move.

"I am not going to hurt you. What would be the point? You are going to be sacrificed, Kairi. The rain will return and Kai will rule May. I knew before we left Mu that you killed Reo. I have waited all this time for your punishment. I can wait one more rise. You think you can control everyone," Ayana sneers, "but you should have been more careful with your pack."

It was over ten orbits ago on the island of Mu where the moon shone bright on the night Reo was forced to disembowel himself. Ikki and Shun returned to their hut unaware a she had watched them greet Kairi and head towards the Mu hill, waiting and hoping to overhear any news about Mu or Takanori.

Ikki and Shun spoke in panicked whispers at what they had seen. Their words just audible to Ayana's straining ears.

"You were lucky he didn't slash you with the sword, you know?" Ikki said, a hysterical note present in his voice.

"I know. Did you see his face when I said 'Send him back with his maymu and keep Ayana and Kai'?" Shun said.

Ikki exhaled. "Good job you didn't say maymu or he would have definitely stabbed you! He is insane, isn't he?"

A silence.

"Oh come on!" Ikki urged Shun. "He's not here now. I thought he couldn't get any crazier than when he destroyed my face with the jellyfish, but all that with Reo was horrible."

Shun sighed. "Yeah. It was. I felt bad for him. I don't think he was asking too much to share the time with his maymu. I mean, what does Kairi think is going to happen? Reo dies and Ayana gives him her maymu?"

"I know," Ikki said, "and what about Kentaro? I can't see him being happy about how obsessed Kairi is with Ayana."

"It's a mess," Shun said.

Ayana had heard enough. And couldn't be certain that she could hold her scream in any longer. She ran to the sea and plunged her head into the water. Screaming until the ocean retreated in fear.

It was a scream that had never really left her, even after ten orbits.

Ayana stands up now and turns away, hot tears stinging her eyes. "He wasn't like you. Reo embraced his mu and was not ashamed of it." Ayana spins around to leer over Kairi. "He was far greater than you! Reo is the he I will raise Kai to be. Not you."

Ayana turns, leans on the wall, and sobs into her palm, sliding down until her back rests against the stone. She cradles her knees and stares at Kairi.

"Maybe I should have ended you then. But I knew for certain I had power over you. And Reo didn't have to die for nothing." Ayana gently rocks back and forth. Her eyes glaze over. "I met them, the other carriers who used to be water hunters, in a cove behind the snake cave on Mu. We would swim from May when you and Kentaro were maiming Maymuans in your pathetic initiation ceremonies." Ayana traces a finger over the raised scar tissue on her arm, remembering her own iniatiation ceremony when Kairi had unleashed a powerful jellyfish on her bare arm.

It was ten orbits ago. Kairi was making final preparations to escape Mu and, unbeknownst to him, Kaori had been swallowed by a snake in the Experienced temple.

"She will be here soon," Ayana said, looking around the cove, avoiding the impatient stares of the other carriers. There was still time. The sun remained high in the sky. They had until its descent to creep back to May.

"Maybe we should begin," urged Miki, casting a furtive look around the cove.

Ayana frowned. Miki's apprehension was unnecessary and annoying. Who would think to look for carriers from May in a hidden cove behind the snake hunt cave?

Splash.

The carriers flinched. Emerging from the water tired but smiling, was Sana.

"We really should find a new place to meet. I am not as comfortable in water as you snake snatchers," Sana said, patting her hair to check her morgon flower was still in place.

The carriers relaxed and Ayana and Sana embraced. Some did not agree with a rural like Sana joining their renegade group but, as Ayana had explained, the task ahead of them required far more willing recruits than only former snake hunters from Ayana's time. They were finite and all who had survived being carriers were present now. Sana had more than proven herself worthy.

"How is Kao?" Ayana asked, her face flushed with a burning intensity.

Sana closed her eyes. "She is safe. How is Kai?"

Ayana gave a tight smile. "Safe."

The two shes squeezed each other's hands tightly.

"Let us begin," Miki said, and led the group to the shore. In a line facing the sea they knelt and placed their palms in the waves that gently lapped the sand.

"Namu Mu Mu."

"Namu Mu Mu."

"Namu Mu Mu."

The group chanted and foam began to appear around Ayana's palms. The water receded a little and a larger wave approached. Still kneeling, the group raised their palms to face the wave as it crashed over them.

They began their discussions. Cleansed.

"What is happening on Mu?" Ayana asked Miki.

"I can't move as freely since my May initiation." Miki grimaced at her freshly lashed arm. She had no choice. The pods were almost ready and she would have been denied entry without visible allegiance. "But I keep it covered with my robe as best I can and Maymuans avoid me anyway. They enjoy sacrifices but don't like to be reminded of sky burials." Miki sneered. "So I know some things."

Ayana raised an eyebrow. "Go on."

"The rearers have discussed going into hiding," Miki said.

The group rustled.

"Why?" Sana snarled. "Have they finally noticed some of them have been dropping dead?"

Miki gave Sana a quizzical look. "Well, yes."

The group exchanged glances of panic.

"What happened?" Ayana asked, face scrunched in concern.

"The last draught you"—Miki paused and searched for the correct word to describe pinning a rearer to the floor of their hut in the depths of darkness before dawn, pulling their jaw apart, and tipping poison down their throat—"administered wasn't strong enough. The rearer wasn't able to say exactly what had happened to her, but she expressed enough to scare the other rearer who found her writhing in agony before she eventually passed."

Ayana kicked up the sand in frustration and the group backed away.

"Don't worry," Sana said, placing her hand on Ayana's mottled arm. "We will find them. There is no place on this island where they can hide from us."

"I know, but it feels like Kairi is almost ready to go wherever it is he plans to go in those pods. We have to execute all the rearers before we leave."

"You won't get all of them," Miki said.

Ayana's eyes flashed with anger. "I will."

"So Kairi still hasn't confided in you where he is going?" Miki asked.

"No."

"Shush. Listen," Sana said, holding her hand up in warning.

Footsteps could be heard slapping the sand on the other side of the snake hunt cave.

"They are coming closer," Sana whispered.

"Don't worry," Ayana said.

"Shush! Now they have gone. That's odd."

Ayana shook her head. "It is Kaori's love, Saki. She enters the cave every rise. She is useful. As long as she continues to come here, we know Kaori has not returned."

Sana looked astonished. "Returned? Returned from where?"

"I don't know exactly what Kairi is planning but it has something to do with Kaori returning. Kentaro is *constantly* talking about Kaori's return."

"But no one has seen her for moons now!" Sana said.

"As far as I know, not since Naho passed." Naho's name caught in Ayana's throat and she bowed to Miki, who accepted her respect.

"I didn't really know Naho but I remember the monsoon." Sana said, and the rest of the group shivered.

"We should still be careful. We don't want Saki to overhear us."

"She is not interested," Ayana said.

Miki's ears pricked up. "What do you mean?"

"I spoke to her," Ayana said.

"You what?" Miki shouted. "Have you been drinking your own draughts? Why would you do such a thing?"

Ayana bristled and stuck her jaw out in an eerie echo of a defiant Kairi. "I still feel something about leaving this ratty island, you know! And when exactly we leave has something to do with Kaori, so I asked Saki if she knew where Kaori was."

Miki rolled her eyes. "As if she would tell you of all Maymuans! You are a *Mayan*."

"That is what she said," Ayana mumbled, digging her toe in the sand to avoid looking at Miki. "I'm sorry. I kind of also wanted to tell her we were doing something," Ayana said quickly. "That we aren't just mindlessly following Kairi."

Only the sound of waves crashing could be heard on the beach.

Sana and Miki stared at each other in shock.

Miki grabbed hold of Ayana's face. "Tell me, right now, that you did not tell Saki about your disloyalty to Kairi."

Ayana wriggled from Miki's grasp. "I didn't have a chance to! As soon as I said Kaori's name she started pointing at my arm and screaming that I had chosen my side. She has no idea what is really going on."

"I hope so, Ayana," Miki said gravely. "You were reckless and put us all in danger."

Ayana looked into each face of the group and knelt before them. "I'm sorry."

"Get up," Miki hissed. "I have more to tell."

Sana pulled Ayana to her feet, shaking her head in disbelief. "Why would you want to tell Saki?"

"I can't describe it. I was waiting for her to approach the cave and I just thought she should know, and Kaori should certainly know, that Kairi is not going to get away with all he has done."

"Then why don't you follow Kaori? Share her fate?" Sana asked.

Ayana looked out across the ocean. "I respect Kaori. Her power is extraordinary. She is water. She can be ferocious and wild, but her true nature is to flow. To soothe. I believe in fighting fire with fire. When lightning strikes, I strike back." Miki frowned but Sana nodded in understanding. Ayana continued, "I couldn't stay with Kaori and watch Kairi sail off in those pods. It is bad enough here on this island with Maymuans who know about their mu. Can you imagine a place with only may?"

"Your may is very pronounced," Miki said, staring into Ayana's eyes.

Ayana flinched. "What is that supposed to mean?"

Miki shrugged. "You would do well to remember the truth. No matter what Kairi says. Forget about 'he' and 'she'. There is only mu and may. We all have both. Mu and may. And we all have a duty to control both our mu and our may."

Ayana and Sana glared at Miki.

"Can I share the rest of my observations now?" Miki asked, and continued without waiting for a reply. "The ankh movement is still alive… I see ankhs etched on the dirt path and many huts still hang a woven ankh by their opening."

"Yes, but what are they doing?" Ayana snapped.

"They are waiting for their leader to return," Miki said calmly.

Ayana screamed in frustration and stomped her foot in the sand. "This is exactly what I mean! Waiting for what? Their island has been ripped apart by a *volcano*. Maymuans are disappearing every rise to join Kairi. The Experienced are hidden away in the temple. They must do something. Now."

"What would you have them do?" Miki asked.

"Anything!" Ayana wailed.

"I have seen many orbits," Miki said, ignoring Ayana's eyeroll. "There is a time for patience. Have you never seen a jungle cat? How they crouch in stillness in order to spring in attack? Or a crocodile? How they lie and wait for the perfect moment to strike?"

"Are they waiting to strike though? Or have they given up and are waiting to be swept away by whatever force ends up being strongest. The flame or the wave?"

Splash.

The group flinched again.

"It's a *he,*" Sana shouted, ready to attack.

"Don't be ridiculous. It's only Reo," Ayana laughed and walked to greet Reo as he exited the ocean.

Ayana flung her arms around Reo's neck and kissed him deeply on his mouth. They parted and gazed into each other's eyes.

"My love," Reo said, taking Ayana's beautiful face in his hands and kissing her again. Ayana led Reo by his hand towards the group.

He was not welcomed; he was tolerated – because of Ayana.

"Are the maymu okay?" Ayana asked.

"You mean mayu?" Reo said gently.

"We don't use that he tongue here!" Sana snapped.

Miki sighed. "He is right. We have to stop speaking as if on Mu. It is not worth the risk of slipping up on May."

The carriers grumbled and Sana glared at Reo.

"How is Kao?" Reo asked, his expression sincere and open to Sana. "Is she okay?"

Sana visibly softened, her shoulders relaxed and she cleared her throat before answering. "Yes, she is okay."

Reo nodded and squeezed Ayana's hand. They smiled at each other.

"They have begun building the initiates' new huts," Reo said.

"Come, we must perform the ceremony and then we have to return," Miki said.

The group returned to the sea.

"Reo could you…?" Ayana began to ask, but Reo was already heading towards the nearest benme to peel off a strip of bark.

In a line facing the horizon, they knelt on the shore. Miki watched the tide carefully. In rhythm with the breath of the sea she chanted, "Namu Mu Mu."

Reo passed the flat benme bark to Ayana then stood beside Miki and chanted, "Namu Mu Mu."

Ayana raised the bark to the sky and said, "May the time we shared be enough. Namu Mu Mu."

She kissed the bark and dipped it into the sea then smeared sand across its surface.

"May we greet in the next. Namu Mu Mu."

Ayana reached up and plucked the red morgon flower from her hair.

"May…" A sob choked the prayer in her mouth. Reo rushed to her side and placed a reassuring hand on her shoulder. Ayana, tears falling, took a deep breath and exhaled.

"May you know me. Namu Mu Mu."

Ayana placed the bark raft on the water. She removed a dagger and bloodstone tucked in her waistband and carefully ignited the flower and dropped it onto the raft.

Ayana dipped her palms into the water and the raft bobbed along the shore, collecting burning flowers and prayers. The raft reached Sana at the end of the line. Rather than chanting "Namu Mu Mu," Sana ignited the flower plucked from her hair and called out to the sea, "For all we lost but will never forget."

Ayana wiped her eyes and focused all her concentration on the smouldering raft.

Slowly it sailed over the unseen bridge in the sea, escaping the push to the shore into the pull of the horizon.

With another splash, the carriers made their journey back to May. Only Miki, Sana, Ayana, and Reo remained in the cove.

Ayana's eyes were still bloodshot from the ceremony. Miki looked to the setting sun then gently stroked her face.

"There is enough time." Miki smiled at Reo and

looked over his shoulder into a cave leading into the cliff. "You can rest a little. Come, Sana."

Sana hesitated but Miki pushed her gently to the water. They entered the water. Sana turned and said, "Ayana?"

Ayana and Reo looked at her in surprise.

"Namu Ayana," Sana said with pride then swam after Miki.

Reo led Ayana to a patch of dry grass beneath a benme. Together they lay. Ayana rested her head on Reo's chest and he stroked her hair.

"Namu Ayana," Reo teased.

Ayana looked up at him and smiled. "Without Sana's courage, what would we have done?"

"I know," Reo sighed and frowned. "How can we ever repay our debt to her?"

They lay listening to the sea caress the shore.

"Do you want to go into the cave?" Reo asked.

"No." Ayana smiled. "I'm happy here."

Reo ran his fingers up and down Ayana's unbranded arm. Ayana stirred and lifted her face to meet his. Slowly she parted his mouth with her tongue. Their shells entwined and for a brief moment May no longer existed.

A knock on the cell door snatches away the thought of Reo and all the sweet memories of the cove.

Ayana scowls and rushes to the door. "What is it?"

"We can't find Kentaro," Miki whispers urgently through the thick door.

Ayana rests her forehead on the wood. "He must be close. He wouldn't leave Kai. Keep looking."

Miki scurries away. Ayana looks down at Kairi and he narrows his eyelids at her.

"Don't get your hopes up," Ayana sneers. "We will find him and he will be executed immediately after you."

Kairi blinks and a tear runs slowly down the side of his face. Ayana kneels beside him and catches it with her finger. She rubs the tear against her thumb.

"He is the only thing you came close to loving, isn't he? But it is not enough. There will be no one to greet you in the next. You were so consumed with power in this time that you forgot about what is needed to transition to the next. Who will guide you? Do you think Takanori will be waiting for you?" Ayana gives a short, sharp laugh. "He used you. You let him suck your soul from your shell. You always thought you were in control but look, here we are, you at my feet. There is still so much you do not know."

Ayana runs her hand down Kairi's cheek, neck, and over his torso until her palm rests flat on his stomach.

"You will never know what it feels like to have a

maymu inside. I have often wondered, if we could all carry, would things have been different?" Ayana sighs and lays her palm on her own stomach. "I don't know; the rearers could carry but they still treated us like boars." Ayana's face cracks. A bitter smile stains her lips and tears tremble in her eyes. "It didn't matter what they did to me. I always loved carrying."

SIXTEEN

Ayana

Mu – Fourteen orbits ago

Hana stirred within Ayana. That was mir name – Hana. If Ayana could choose, and if it was a maymu who could never carry, Ayana would have called mem Rui. But Ayana couldn't choose. Mu was heavily carrying in the rearer clearing deep within Mu's jungle, surrounded by other full bloom carriers.

"Ayana." The rearer smiled. "It's time for your cleanse."

A narrow stream gurgled through the clearing. The rearer gently removed Ayana's robe, carefully untying the obi that rested on mir bump. Ayana lay in the stream. The water soothed mir aching lower back. The rearer gently washed Ayana's face, arms, and chest with a sea sponge.

Footsteps approached and another rearer proceeded to smash and grind mimin seeds to extract oil to rub into Ayana's skin.

"Open," the rearer said.

Ayana hesitated.

The rearer glared. "I said, *open*."

Ayana's knees parted and the rearer wiped the sponge between mir legs. The mimin rearer stopped grinding.

"Look," the washing rearer said with excitement, holding the sponge out for the other to see. "It is, isn't it?"

The mimin rearer peered at the sponge. "Maybe?"

"It's not," Ayana said. They looked down at mem in surprise. Mu knew what they were looking for; the tiny jellyfish that kept the maymu sealed up inside. Its appearance was a sign that the maymu was imminent. "I know; I have given the island two maymu already."

"It is too small," the washing rearer conceded, "but it could have broken into pieces. I have seen that happen before. Have you noticed anything else leave your shell?"

The two rearers stared at Ayana.

"No," Ayana lied. Mu had decided; Hana may be given to the island but mu was going to deliver mem. Not the rearers. Seven rises ago, Hana had unplugged the jellyfish, warning Ayana to be ready. Then Ayana had woken this rise with spots of blood on mir benme mat.

Mu had quickly flipped it over and wiped the speckles of red from mir thighs. Hana was coming.

The washing rearer said, "After we massage mem, we should use the last of the oil for a sweep."

Ayana, now lying on the grass beside the stream, felt panic rise inside mem. They had swept mem last time. If they used their fingers to try and bring on the maymu, mu might not be able to hide that Hana was ready to breathe on Mu.

The rearers began to massage the oil into Ayana's skin. Mu had to distract them.

"What is your name?"

The washing rearer scowled. The mimin-grinding rearer flicked away Ayana's question with mir hand but still answered, "We don't have names."

"But you must have had a naming ceremony."

The two rearers exchanged a glance.

"Yes," began the mimin-grinding rearer but the washing rearer injected.

"Enough."

The massage continued with only the sound of a squawking buha and the tinkle of the stream navigating smooth pebbles. The rearers worked swiftly until they were both massaging Ayana's stomach.

"Oh," the washing rearer gasped, "the maymu kicked me!"

"Really? Namu May Mu!" the mimin rearer squealed

in delight, but then mir face fell as suddenly and as startlingly as a loud clap of thunder.

"What's wrong?" the washing rearer asked.

The mimin rearer snatched mir hands away from Ayana's stomach. "I felt a kick this side too."

"You can't have. How could it have kicked both sides?"

The rearers looked at each other and watched the blood drain from each other's faces.

"We will have to warn the Experienced."

Ayana tried to sit up but as mu did – *pop* – mir thighs flooded with the fluid of mir womb.

The rearers gasped.

Four rearers pinned Ayana down on mir back. A fifth peered between mir legs and barked, "Push."

"Please," Ayana pleaded, "let me stand. Not like this. I can't do it like this … please."

The rearer glared at Ayana. "Push now. It is your island duty."

Ayana tried to writhe free. The rearers squeezed mir wrists and pulled mir ankles further apart.

Ayana wanted to keep Hana inside. It was the only way to hold mem close, to keep mem, for just one more moment, but mu could feel the skull bearing down. The waves Hana sailed were crashing closer and closer together. With the next swell, Ayana allowed memself to be swept away, even though mu knew in this position that mu was going to tear.

The wail of a fresh maymu pierced the dense foliage surrounding the clearing. The rearers released Ayana and focused on the maymu.

"Hana!" Ayana screamed, mir arms reaching out. "Give mu to me."

The rearer wrapping the maymu hissed, "Mir name is not Hana."

"Hana!" Ayana screamed, and scrambled to mir feet. A deep, powerful voice distracted mem from snatching Hana from the rearer.

"You have fulfilled your island duty. You may feel pride." Ayana stared at Takanori in confusion. Why was mu here? Ayana had never seen mem in the rearer clearing before. Mu hadn't been there when Ayana's previous two maymus entered Mu. Before mu could fathom a reason, the ocean inside mem stirred again and another wave crashed. Ayana seized hold of Takanori's shoulders in surprise. Staring into mir face, as craggy as the bark on the tree stumps hacked down to make the unnatural clearing, Ayana felt a second skull descend.

The rearers rushed to try and unhook Ayana from Takanori but mu commanded they leave mem alone. Hanging from mir neck, Ayana writhed and moaned until instinct bent mir knees into a deep squat and mu guided the maymu from mir shell.

It was one would could never carry.

Ayana picked mem up, held mem close to mir chest and murmured, "Rui."

Time in the clearing ended. Takanori and the rearers were momentarily suspended, unable to interrupt a carrier and mir maymu.

Hana, still wrapped up tight but now lying on the grass momentarily forgotten, began to wail. Mir cry shattered time.

Takanori snatched Rui from Ayana's embrace and the rearers seized Ayana. Takanori stared, transfixed, at the maymu. Rui peered back into the face which had seen so many orbits. Takanori ran mir wrinkled finger across Rui's taut skin, wiping away a smudge of Ayana's blood.

Ayana and Hana's screams continued to rattle the clearing. Takanori accepted a cloth held out to mem by a rearer and wrapped Rui up tight. Only then did Rui begin to cry, rebelling against the restraint. A shadow crossed Takanori's brow and mu no longer gazed at the maymu in wonder.

Ayana watched in horror as two figures shrouded in black robes approached Rui. As they reached Takanori, their faces became clear. Ayana gasped. It was death. The two who shadow the Experienced after sacrifices. Ayana had seen them recently, when the farmers were sacrificed for the locust plague. Miki and Naho. Some say they can speak nabgar. Some say Miki is a nabgar soul in a violated shell.

Naho reached out for Rui and Takanori handed mem over. Miki knelt down and scooped up Hana from the floor. Without a backwards glance, they turned to re-enter the gloom of the surrounding forest, Takanori in their wake.

"Rui! Hana!" Ayana screamed. Mu escaped from the clutches of the rearers but in mir haste tripped and lay sprawled on the floor, "Rui! Hana!"

The rearers tried to drag Ayana to mir feet but mu clung to the dark earth, tears soaking mir face, mir eyes frantic and wild. "Rui! Hana!"

Takanori returned to leer over Ayana. "You cannot return until you forget."

The strangeness of Takanori's words momentarily silenced Ayana but when Rui and Hana disappeared into the forest, Ayana shattered again and shards of mir soul exploded across the clearing.

"Rui! Hana!"

The rearers dragged Ayana from the clearing by mir ankles. Mir fingernails raked the earth, desperate to leave a trail for Rui and Hana to find their way back to mem.

SEVENTEEN

Ayana

Mu – Fourteen orbits ago

The following rise Ayana woke up in an unfamiliar hut. The door creaked open and sunlight reluctantly entered. Ayana stirred, mir lips dry and cracked; mir jaw aching from grinding mir teeth.

"Water," the rearer said, placing a small woven cup in the thin sunbeam. At the sound of what mu needed most, Ayana scuttled on mir hands and knees towards the light. The rearer swiftly closed the door and the hut was plunged back into darkness. Disoriented, Ayana reached for the water but it wasn't there. Knowing the water would be leaking from the poorly woven cup, mu scrambled around trying to find it. The back of mir hand struck the cup and it toppled over. With a wail, Ayana quickly brought it to mir lips but it barely wet mir tongue. Desperate, mu wiped mir palm on the wet, dusty floor and sucked as much moisture as mu could from mir fingers.

"Water," the rearer said again the following rise. Ayana curled up tighter into mir corner. The door opened wide and Ayana squinted into the light.

"How can you do this to a Maymuan who shares your shell?" Ayana rasped.

The rearer sucked mir teeth. "We may share a shell but we are not of the same mind. Why didn't you just take the nimi root? Then none of this would have happened."

"Where are Rui and Hana?" Ayana asked.

"There is no Rui and there is no Hana," the rearer said.

Ayana opened mir mouth and a sob soared out of mir throat. It passed Ayana's cracked lips and grew in size, filling the space until there was barely room for Ayana's shell. The rearer could not endure the sound and slammed the hut door shut and bolted it from the outside.

"Water." Ayana reached towards the sliver of light, drained the cup, then threw it at the rearer.

"How many maymu did you create?" the rearer asked, ignoring the cup.

"I have two maymus!"

The rearer shook mir head in exasperation and closed the door behind mem.

Ayana leapt up and pounded on the bolted door. "I have two maymus! Rui and Hana! And nothing you ratty do to me will ever change that! Why can the twins Kaori and Kairi live but Rui and Hana can not?"

"Water." Ayana's hair hung in lank clumps around mir face. Mir skin was itchy and dirty. Mir stomach had long stopped rumbling. If the arrival of the water came once per rise, then mu had been in the hut for at least thirty rises.

"How many maymus did you create?"

"One," Ayana said.

The door slammed shut. The cries of Rui and Hana replaced the silence. Ayana's shell leaked milk despite mir dehydration, the urge to soothe mir maymus too great. Ayana resumed banging mir forehead against the wooden wall until mu woke and found memself sprawled on the floor.

"Water."

"Thank you."

"How many maymus did you create?"

"I did not create any maymus this time."

The rearer smiled. "I will send a rural."

The hut door closed softly.

Ayana traced the grain in the wooden panels of the hut walls with mir fingertip. The door creaked open and sunlight poured into the space. Ayana squinted at the two figures silhouetted by the sun.

"This is Sana," the rearer said. "Mu is going to return you to the island."

Ayana tried to enter the grain, tried to force mir finger, hand, arm, then entire shell into the vein of the wood where mu could feel safe.

A figure approached. Ayana's shell trembled and flinched when a hand touched mir shoulder.

"I am Sana."

The voice was soft, a caress not a command. Ayana peered up, curious. She saw a Maymuan who looked the same number of orbits as memself. Sana gently brushed

Ayana's dirty matted hair from mir face and Ayana closed mir eyes and softly sighed.

"Mu must return by the seventh rise." The rearer barked at Sana, who nodded. Ayana scurried back into the wall.

"This door will no longer be locked," The rearer pointed to the light outside. "Do you want to leave now?"

The rearer and Sana watched Ayana carefully. Mu peered over mir shoulder to the open door, shuddered, then resumed gazing into the wall.

The rearer scoffed—"They never do."—and walked out, leaving the door ajar.

Sana watched the rearer leave.

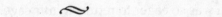

Rise One

"I know it's hard but try to drink only the milk," Sana said, watching Ayana scrape mir teeth furiously against the coco pulp. Ayana cracked another coco open, slurped the milk, and again tried to eat as much coco flesh as possible.

Sana tutted and waited. The sound of gnawing abruptly ended and was replaced by retching. Sana hurried to help Ayana as mir stomach rejected the unfamiliar food.

"Don't worry," Sana said, stroking Ayana's dirty hair from mir face. "You will enjoy them again. But for now, please only the milk and a handful of the grubs I have toasted."

Ayana wiped mir lips with the back of mir hand and grabbed a handful of the plump insects Sana had prepared. Mu shoved them in mir mouth and glared at Sana.

They sat surveying each other in the shadow of Ayana's cage. The rearer's instructions were clear; six rises, then on the seventh Ayana must attend the temple and face the Experienced.

"I want to go back in there," Ayana mumbled through the half-chewed grubs,

Sana glanced at the hut and frowned, saddened that Ayana was so eager to return to mir cage.

"Okay, but first you must let me bathe you." Ayana flinched and wrapped mir arms around memself, while Sana gestured to the bucket beside mem. "We can do it here. We don't have to go to the stream. Okay?"

Ayana glanced up at Sana and then hugged memself even tighter.

"Will you change robes?" Sana held up a clean gobu robe. No reply. Sana sighed. "I'm just going to wipe your face and arms for now then, okay?"

Ayana nodded.

Sana looked at Ayana's matted hair, surely alive with

ants, and mu looked at the robe encrusted with dust and the neckline stained with blood from the split in Ayana's forehead. It would have to wait for another rise. The sea sponge Sana dipped into the bucket soaked up the clear stream water. Gently, Sana wiped the dried blood staining Ayana's eyebrows and the dust that was stuck to mir cheeks. The cool water in the sponge soaked Sana's palm but mu felt a sudden heat on the back of mir hand. Hot tears splashed on mir skin.

"It's okay," Sana whispered to Ayana. "It's going to be okay."

Ayana leaned into Sana and they embraced. The water bucket abandoned, Sana scooped Ayana up and carried mem into the hut.

"Don't shut the door," Ayana said, curling into the wood that was stained with mir blood.

"Okay."

"And don't leave."

Sana paused at the opening. Mu turned and saw Ayana was watching mem.

"I won't," Sana said and lay down beside the opening.

Rise Two

Sana tugged the wide-toothed wooden comb through

Ayana's resistant mane. The bucket, replenished many times by Sana, was now only a little cloudy from the dirt rinsed from Ayana's hair. The first rinse had made the water a swamp.

But still the comb refused to pass through Ayana's hair.

"I'm just going to crush some mimin," Sana said, rummaging in mir pocket for the seeds. As Sana ground the seeds, a rage trembled Ayana's shell as mu thought of the massage mu received from the rearers by the stream.

"I think that is enough," Sana said, peering into the oil then looking up to check Ayana's hair again. "Are you okay?" mu asked, noticing the expression on Ayana's face.

"Yes," Ayana snarled. "Do you have any more draught?"

Sana frowned. Mu had remained with Ayana throughout the night but mir presence did not bring Ayana the comfort mu so desperately craved. Ayana physically fought mir dreams, thrashing and wailing into the night. Sana, as all rurals do, had the knowledge of the trees and the land, and mu had made Ayana a root draught for a dreamless sleep.

"I can make you more when the sun sets," Sana said carefully, "but for now let me soak your hair with this oil and comb out the last of the ants."

Ayana couldn't help but scratch mir scalp. Sana began rubbing the oil into Ayana's long hair.

"That draught you made," Ayana said.

"Yes…" Sana answered warily. Mir island duty was to return Ayana back to Mu, not to reveal all the secrets of the rurals.

"What root did you use?"

Sana paused in combing Ayana's hair. "Different roots have different effects. I used a root to help you sleep."

"But if you boiled more of that same root would I sleep … deeper?"

Ayana turned to face Sana.

"Deeper?" Sana dropped the comb and stared into Ayana's eyes. "Do you want to rest, Ayana?"

"Yes," Ayana said, breaking Sana's gaze and staring into the grass.

"I am a rural," Sana said, running mir fingers over the blades of grass protruding from the red earth. "There is a tree near the preparer hut. Once an orbit, for ten maybe twelve rises, the most beautiful buds bloom. We can't eat them, or drink them – they don't even have a strong smell – but they are beautiful. We call them momu momu. Without the blooms the tree looks like an empty shell. Every moon until they bloom again the rurals fight with the preparers. The preparers forget the beauty and the wonder of the unfurl and want to chop the tree down and plant something they consider more useful. But nowhere else does this type of tree bloom on Mu. Have you ever seen the momu momu in bloom?"

Ayana shook mir head.

"Then there is still much more for you to see in this time." Sana reached out for Ayana's hand. "We are Maymuans. We must speak with the tongues of the Experienced or sew our lips shut. My island duty is to return carriers to Mu. Most remain whole, particularly the zealous, and only need rest and food. But those whom I greet in that hut"—Sana shivered—"are broken."

Ayana's head flicked up to look at Sana and mir hand squeezed Sana's tightly.

Sana leaned into Ayana's face. "I don't know what they do to you, but my life is of the land. I nurture beauty but I have also observed enough beasts to know it is something wicked."

Ayana's eyes shone for the first time since escaping the hut. Mu was seen. Sana saw mem.

"And," Sana continued, mir voice a hiss, "I don't think it is you who deserves to be drinking potent draughts. Do you?"

Rise Three

Ayana paced around the hut sipping from a pierced coco.

"Do you want some of this?" Ayana asked.

Sana paused in roasting the spiders on the small fire pit. "No, I will pluck some more later. You should finish it."

Ayana drained the last of the sweet, warm milk. "Can I roast the inside?"

"Yes, sure. Do you want me to crack it?"

"I can do it," Ayana said, squatting over a large rock. First mu brought the coco down slowly to the edge of the rock and then mu lifted the coco high above her head and brought it down with an almighty force. The coco shattered and shards of shell and pulp exploded across the grass.

Sana raised an eyebrow. "Feel better?"

Ayana smiled a little. "No."

Sana smiled. "These are almost ready. Keep an eye on them. Let's see if any of your coco is salvageable."

Ayana stared at the spiders roasting in the pit, the hairs on the legs crackling and sparkling in the flame.

"I am not going to be fixed by the seventh rise."

"Of course not," Sana said, sprinkling the shattered chunks of coco mu had collected into the pit. "You are a Maymuan. You will pretend."

Sana laid two benme leaves down beside the pit and handed Ayana a long, pointed stick.

"The spiders are ready."

Ayana impaled the spiders one by one until there was a small pile on each leaf.

"And the coco is ready too."

They sat beside each other eating their meal, crunching crispy spider legs.

"I am not going to be fixed in seven orbits, never mind seven rises," Ayana said, tears stinging her eyes.

Sana quickly swallowed the spider mu had been chewing. "Now that we don't know."

"I know," Ayana snapped, launching the stick into the pit. The pointed end speared deep into the ashes, sparing the other end the ordeal of the fire. Flames licked the wood until the whole stick burnt and collapsed into the fire pit. "There are wounds in this time that can never be healed."

They watched the stick become ash.

"Yet you will still be here, Ayana," Sana said gently.

"But they won't," Ayana snarled.

"Who?"

Ayana shook mir head.

"Who won't be here?" Sana insisted, mir eyes narrowing.

The benme leaf of spiders on Ayana's lap tumbled to the ground. Mu leaped up and marched into the hut.

After collecting the fallen spiders and wrapping them carefully in the leaf, Sana followed Ayana into the hut.

Mu gasped. Mu had been expecting Ayana to be huddled against the wall or maybe whacking mir forehead against the wood, but Ayana was standing in the middle of the hut, staring at mem.

Sana hesitated but approached. "Here, try and eat these. You need them."

"What did the others say?"

A heavy breath exhaled from Sana's mouth. "The other carriers in this hut? Not much. But enough."

"What do they do with them?"

Sana swallowed the rusty water that had flooded mir mouth. Ayana reminded mem of a boar before it charged.

"I don't know."

"What have they done with my maymus?" Ayana roared.

"I..." Sana took a step back towards the opening.

Ayana slumped down to the floor. "I saw death take them."

"Then in death you may find the answer. But first you must become strong," Sana said, reaching out a hand to the extraordinary carrier before mem. Ayana took it and Sana led mem back outside into the falling dusk.

"Eat."

The benme unwrapped, all that could be heard beside the hut bathed in silver moonlight was the determined crunch of coco and spider.

Rise Four

"You don't need to fill the bucket. I will come to the stream."

Sana smiled and placed the bucket back on the grass. Together they walked from the clearing towards the tinkle of flowing water.

At the bank, Ayana removed mir new clean robe and eased memself into the river. Mu flinched as the cool water stung the tears mu had from delivering mir maymus. Sana hurried away to collect guma leaves.

"It will be best if you chew these yourself and then place them on your wound," Sana said.

Ayana left the stream and wrapped the gobu robe around mir wet shell.

"While you chew may I croprow your hair?" Sana asked.

Ayana sat between Sana's legs and mir curls were combed and tamed, the Maymuan way.

"I can't," Ayana hesitated. "I can't quite get this where it needs to be."

Sana crawled around to face Ayana and accepted the chewed guma. Ayana's knees remained squeezed shut.

"Whenever you are ready, open a little and I will apply it. Okay?"

"Okay," Ayana murmured.

The stream gurgled beside them and in the quiet the sweet trill of girnums rustled the leaves.

Ayana opened enough for Sana to soothe mem then lay down to rest a little while Sana rinsed mir hands in the stream.

~

"We should return soon." Sana said, gazing at the red sun ready to descend into the trees. With a yawn Ayana sat up and looked around, disorientated,

"Where are we?"

"You had a little rest."

Ayana pointed up at the red sky. "It was more than a little!"

Sana shrugged and passed Ayana a coco to sip.

"I was thinking," Sana began cautiously, "about chanting."

"I don't want to chant Namu May Mu," Ayana snapped, throwing the coco into the grass.

"Okay, but how about something else?"

"What do you mean?" Ayana asked.

"You know what we spoke of in the last rise? I was thinking maybe we could send a message to your"—Sana closed mir eyes—"maymus."

Ayana's eyes narrowed.

"Just something simple," Sana said quickly. "Look."

Sana waved a benme leaf and crouched beside the stream. Ayana reluctantly sat beside mem.

Raising the leaf to the sky Sana said, "May the time we shared be enough."

Sana dipped the leaf in the stream. "May we greet in the next."

Smearing a handful of soil across the leaf, Sana swallowed and whispered, "May you know me."

Ayana did not blink. Wide-eyed, mu watched as the leaf set sail down the stream. When it could no longer be seen Sana placed mir hand on Ayana's shoulder but Ayana swatted it away.

"You have no right."

"Sorry?" Sana said, confused.

"How dare you!" Ayana screamed. "How ratty dare you! Stay away from me. You are as wicked as them."

Sana stood, helpless, as Ayana dived into the concealment of the forest.

Rise Five

The mango and roasted boar meat Sana had prepared before succumbing to sleep had gone. Sana decided to take this as a good sign. Ayana had returned, as had mir appetite. With a sigh, Sana headed towards the stream. Mu hoped to find Ayana, and soon, because experience told mem a rearer was imminent to inspect their progress.

Relief flooded Sana when mu spotted Ayana kneeling beside the stream. Sana rushed forward but froze when mu realised Ayana was placing a benme leaf on the water. Sana watched, astonished, as Ayana crawled into the stream, mir knees and hands submerged. Sana shivered when mu realised that the benme leaf, rather than flowing downstream, was floating suspended between Ayana's submerged palms. The leaf then began to sail against the current, gliding upstream, rebelling against the natural flow.

Sana gasped and Ayana whipped mir hands from the water. The stream snatched the leaf and ignored Ayana's desperate attempt to rescue it. Mu had no choice but to let it go and watch the leaf tumble downstream in the eternal rhythm of the current.

"How did you do that?" Sana asked.

Ayana scowled. "I was a water hunter."

Sana's eyebrows shot up in surprise. "Can all water hunters do what you just did?"

"Probably," Ayana said dismissively, wringing the water from the bottom of mir robe. "Why are you here? Can't you just leave me alone? Even for one rise?"

"I'm expecting a rearer."

Ayana's face hardened.

"We should wait by the hut," Sana said.

They walked to the hut in silence. Sana stole glances at Ayana but mir jaw was set so firmly that mu didn't dare try and speak to mem.

Sana saw the hut first and squeezed Ayana's wrist in warning. "They are here."

Peering into the embers of the fire and murmuring to each other were two rearers.

"Namu May Mu," Sana said,

The rearers looked up in surprise. "Namu May Mu," they replied in unison.

The rearer – whom Sana and Ayana had last seen walking away from the unlocked hut – approached. Sana instinctively took a step closer to Ayana.

The rearer scowled. "You need to report," mu barked, nodding in the direction of the other rearer. "I will check the carrier."

"Ayana," Sana said as mu passed the rearer.

"What?" the rearer asked, frowning.

"Mir name is Ayana."

The rearer narrowed mir eyes and watched Sana greet the other rearer. Mu blinked and shook mir head as if to free memself from a swarm of flies, then marched towards Ayana.

The rearer pinched Ayana's chin between mir fingers and thumb and tilted Ayana's head so mu could inspect mir face.

"You need to apply more guma to your head," the rearer said, wrinkling mir nose in distaste at the welt on Ayana's forehead, "but other than that, Sana has done well." The rearer glanced at Sana and sucked mir teeth. "Mu gets too attached of course, but mu fulfils mir island duty well." Fortunately, the rearer was too absorbed in mir own musings to notice the hatred dripping from Ayana's pores.

"Okay, take off your robe."

"No."

The rearer was forced to look at Ayana. "Did you hear what I said? Take off your robe."

Ayana wrapped the robe tighter around mir shell. "No."

The rearer reached out to rip open the robe but Ayana swatted mir hand away.

"What's going on?" Sana asked, stepping between the two.

"I need to inspect the shell."

"It's fine," Sana said.

The rearer laughed, a short sharp snort. "I will decide."

Leaves that had lain too close to the fire crunched underfoot as the other rearer approached. "Mu does seem well. What rise is this, Sana?"

"Five."

The angry rearer exhaled loudly, blowing hot air

through mir teeth; the other rearer raised mir eyebrows in encouragement at Sana.

"I have applied guma to mir tears every rise," Sana said, ignoring Ayana shift uncomfortably behind mem. "Mu will be ready for the temple. Namu May Mu. Namu Experienced."

The angry rearer glared but allowed memself to be led away by the other.

When the squabbling of the rearers returning to Mu could no longer be heard, Ayana said, "I can never see Takanori. I want to stick my nails into mir eyes."

Sana flinched. "You can see mem. And you won't do that."

"Why did you lie?" Ayana snapped.

"About what?"

"About applying the guma every rise. You have only applied it once by the stream."

"Why wouldn't you let mem take off your robe?" Sana asked.

Ayana looked at Sana and chewed mir lip to stop the words pouring out.

Sana nodded brusquely. "I lied for the same reason. Now tell me, what do you need to be ready for the Experienced temple?"

Ayana stopped chewing mir lip. "I need Reo."

"Who is Reo?"

"My pair."

Sana had thought mu had seen and heard everything in this clearing.

"You look surprised," Ayana said.

"No carrier has ever asked me for their pair."

Ayana pondered this for a moment. "Then I am sad for them."

"I will bring mem on the next rise," Sana agreed.

"Can't I go to mem?"

"No."

Ayana frowned a little but accepted Sana's answer. Mu began collecting sticks to reignite the fire, a lightness in mir step Sana had not seen until now.

Who is this Reo? Sana thought, *and what had mu done to earn this beautiful carrier's heart?*

Rise Six

Ayana paced around the hut waiting for Sana to return, hopefully with Reo. Mir mind raced. Mir eyes darted into the green of the forest eager for any sign of mem. For calm mu closed mir eyes and thought of their journey to create Hana and Rui. The caress of the warm sun on mir shoulders as Reo held out mir hand to help mem scale the mountain. The tinkle of strips of seashells swaying in the breeze as they approached the creation hut opening. Reo's mouth, warm on mers as they enjoyed being far away from all other Maymuans. Alone, together. They may have been forced together by the Experienced at their pairing ceremony but Ayana and Reo's love was true.

Ayana opened mir eyes and stared into the forest. Branches swayed gently, their leaves a rhythmic rustle counting the moments before Ayana would see mem. Ayana stared into the dark space between the trees. Where was mu? And then, there mu was. Ayana blinked and still Reo remained. Ayana had thought mu would skip but mir legs remained as still as the tree trunks surrounding mem, mir feet rooted firmly in the ground.

Reo sprinted to Ayana and ran mir fingers over the tight croprows Sana had sown. Reo gently stroked the damaged skin on mir forehead. Reo tried to kiss Ayana's mouth but mu was horrified to find Reo didn't feel how mu had in mir dreams. Mir tongue felt intrusive. Reo cupped Ayana's face in mir hands and kissed Ayana's forehead, cheeks and chin instead until Sana cleared mir throat.

They parted and Ayana, finally able to move, stepped away from mem so Ayana, Reo, and Sana stood in an awkward pyramid shape. Reo glanced from Ayana to Sana and frowned. This wasn't how Ayana thought it would be at all. Mu sighed heavily and leaned against the hut for support. Reo made to step towards Ayana but mu shook mir head quickly and Reo froze.

"What is going on here?" Reo asked,

Ayana and Sana exchanged a look.

"Ayana?" Reo said in exasperation, "What is happening? Are you okay? This rearer came for me."

"Mu is not a rearer," Ayana snapped.

Reo held up mir palms in surrender, "Okay. This…"

"My name is Sana."

Reo stared at mem and then returned to addressing Ayana: "Sana, told me to follow mem and that mu would lead me to you."

Ayana scowled.

"Why are you looking at me like that?" Reo sobbed. "I don't understand."

"I…" Ayana faltered and then mir scowl deepened. "Why did you think Sana was a rearer?"

Reo glanced at Sana. "I'm not sure I can answer that now, Ayana."

Ayana looked from Reo to Sana. "Say it."

Reo swallowed. "I know what happened here."

Ayana was glad mu was already leaning against the hut. Mir hand slapped mir mouth, trying to catch mir gasp.

Sana's eyes narrowed. "Know what?"

Reo checked for permission to speak again from Ayana. Mu nodded, "A rearer came to my hut. They told me that we had not been successful in fulfilling our island duty."

Sana and Ayana stared at Reo, stunned.

"I suppose that is one way of phrasing it," Sana muttered.

Reo continued. "I was surprised. Why did they have to come and tell me? Why didn't you come?"

Ayana looked into Reo, still lost for words.

"I know this must be terrible for you, Ayana, but I need to know what happened," Reo continued. "All the rearer said was that the maymu did not survive the passing from you to Mu."

The grain of the wood in the hut walls tugged at Ayana. If mu could just tuck memself inside, then mu would no longer have to live this time with these words ringing in mir ears.

Reo shuffled impatiently. Mu knew better than to approach Ayana but mu could not hide mir frustration. "Are you okay, Ayana? Please speak to me. I need to hear you. Please. Say anything!"

Ayana twisted mir entire shell around and laid mir palms and forehead on the hut. Mu looked like an Experienced whispering into the chalky cliff during a snake hunt.

"This was a mistake. You need to leave," Sana said, tugging on Reo's arm.

Reo brushed Sana off. "I'm not leaving. Not until one of you tells me what the ratty hell is going on here?"

"Look at mem," Sana hissed. "If you love mem, leave."

Reo hesitated, torn between Ayana and the forest.

"Ayana? Can I stay? Even for a little? We don't have to talk anymore. Just let me…" Reo sobbed into mir fist. "Just let me hold you."

"No," Ayana said, without turning.

Reo stared at Ayana's back then swung around to face Sana. Mu trembled at the pain stained across Reo's face. "I don't understand. Help me. Please help me."

Sana placed a gentle palm on Reo's shoulder. Mir shell caved inwards. Sana ran mir hand down Reo's arm until mir palm was in mers. "Come."

Reo allowed Sana to draw mem towards the forest but mir eyes never left Ayana.

"I can't leave mem like this," Reo pleaded.

"I shouldn't have taken you from the preparers' hut. It was my mistake."

"How can I leave mem?"

Sana sighed. "You're a preparer, right?"

Reo nodded, baffled by the question at this time.

"Mu will return and when mu does, please show mem the momu momu tree in bloom."

Reo stared at Sana. "You're a rural."

"I am. My island duty is to return Ayana. I will fulfil my island duty."

With a sigh, Reo said, "The only sight I have ever seen

on Mu equal to the beauty of the momu momu is Ayana."

Sana nodded, mir eyes stinging with fresh tears. "I promise you will have your chance to show mem."

Sana watched Reo reluctantly leave and mu returned to the hut and peeled Ayana from the side.

They sat, Sana cradling Ayana as Ayana had cradled Rui.

"Will you ever tell mem what really happened to your maymus?" Sana asked, stroking Ayana's scalp.

Hot tears flooded Sana's robe. "If I am to live, then first I must decide what I am going to tell myself. Maybe Reo's version will ensure I survive."

Sana stopped stroking Ayana. "Listen to me very carefully. It is always easier to live in truth. Even in a place such as this, which demands we lie to those around us. Even if it is only you who breathes the truth. You are enough. I have watched carriers return to Mu from this hut. Those who try to deny rot faster than ganba plucked from its stalk. They are the ones whose shells hang empty in the cob fields."

Ayana shivered.

~

Rise Seven

"I don't remember you as an unnamed but our shells

are similar," Ayana said as they approached the temple. It was time for Ayana to face the Experienced.

"I don't remember you either. I think I have lived a few more orbits," Sana replied.

"Although we look the same, you know so much more about Mu than I do. You know about everything!" Ayana said.

"Not everything." Sana smiled. "But I am fortunate to be a rural. To have observed the skies and the land every rise has nourished my soul."

"I wish I were a rural."

Sana stared at Ayana. "I am in awe of the courage of water hunters. I could not do what you do."

Ayana sighed.

"I mean it, Ayana. The eternal training of the water hunter has given you a courage few on Mu will ever know."

"Why didn't you become a carrier?" The question burst out of Ayana.

Sana gestured to the gold doors of the temple. "We are here. You must enter alone."

"I will. But first tell me, why didn't you become a carrier?"

Sana cast a furtive look around and answered simply, "I didn't want to."

"What do you mean you didn't want to?" Ayana shrieked in surprise.

"Lower your voice. You know where we are." Ayana blushed and Sana continued, "I was paired but every rise I chewed the nimi root. Eventually it was decided I was incapable of carrying and I was given the island duty of returning carriers from the rearer clearing."

"If the Experienced thought you couldn't carry, why didn't they make you a rearer?"

"I don't know. I was fortunate they needed me to care for carriers. I could not be a rearer," Sana added with a scowl.

Ayana pondered what Sana had said. "Do you think all the rearers chewed the nimi root?"

"I am sure most did but there must also be some who just couldn't create. Perhaps they are the ones who are a little kinder and less judgemental. I don't know." Sana shrugged.

"But you know what that means?" Ayana said, eyes shining, "If you survive enough orbits, you could become an Experienced!"

Sana laughed. "Hopefully there will no longer be Experienced by the time I could become one."

"What do you mean?"

"You seem to take everything as fixed. I watch the leaves on a tree: they unfurl, shrivel, fall, feed the tree, and soon another sprouts. You see the same leaf; I see change. The cycle is eternal but no two leaves are exactly the same."

Ayana frowned.

"Look," Sana said, pointing at the sun dipping towards the land. "It is time."

Ayana made to push the gold doors open. Sana seized mir hand. "Not that way."

Sana led Ayana around the temple to a concealed entrance with a discreet thick wooden door.

"So many secrets," Ayana muttered.

Sana murmured in agreement, "But you know, despite all I have seen, I still miss my time as an unnamed."

Ayana didn't respond.

"I was so happy to leave the rearers and be surrounded with others of the same orbit every single rise. Maybe this is why we are all so willing to obey the Experienced. We all loved our time in the temple so much."

"I didn't," Ayana said. "I have no memory of rearers and living with them in the forest. I can remember darkness. And water."

"What are you saying?" Sana asked, confused. "That you weren't with the rearers? Where were you then? It doesn't make any sense."

"I know," Ayana said, shaking mir head in frustration. "I can remember feeling afraid of the temple and not wanting to leave where I was. It's so strange."

"Did you recognise anyone when you entered the

temple? There would have been at least a few unnamed from your rearer group."

"No."

Sana stared at Ayana. "How can that be?"

"I don't know." Ayana shrugged. Mu was more concerned about what awaited mem behind the secret door. "Should I go in now?"

"Yes," Sana answered, still perplexed by what Ayana had said. "Follow the scent of burning humir. Push the door beneath the inlaid shell and the Experienced will be waiting."

Ayana passed through the secret door and Sana closed it softly behind mem then laid mir forehead on the wood and chanted "Namu May Mu."

EIGHTEEN

Ayana

Mu – Fourteen orbits ago

Ayana entered the Experienced chamber. The fire pits crackled and flickered, illuminating the twelve ganba thrones. Perched on each was an Experienced shrouded in immaculate red robes with their long silver braids knotted on their heads. Takanori narrowed mir eyes and watched Ayana walk slowly to the centre of the chamber.

"You may kneel," Takanori said when Ayana reached the centre.

Ayana glared at mem but did not refuse. Mu lowered memself slowly to the ground, heart pounding. Ayana's eyes swept the twelve Experienced. Cold, dark eyes surveyed mem as a nabgar would its prey. The only warmth was in the flicker of flame within the fire pits, beside which was a small basin of water to extinguish the fire when necessary. Ayana drank in the water and felt mir heart calm.

Takanori scratched mir long index fingernail across the arm of mir throne and began, "Namu May Mu."

"Namu May Mu," the assembled Experienced echoed and Ayana muttered.

"Namu Experienced."

"Namu Experienced!" the Experienced roared and Ayana flinched.

"Ayana. You were unsuccessful in fulfilling your island duty."

Ayana felt mir jaw tighten. Takanori glanced at the water basin. The water had begun to bubble. Ayana closed mir eyes and whatever Takanori said next mu did not hear. Instead the water in the basin bubbled over and continued to flow until the red hems of all the Experienced were soaked. They remained seated; they were not afraid of a little water. Ayana smiled. The water continued to rise and it was too late when the Experienced thought to flee. Ayana stood dry in the centre of the chamber as the water swirled and swept them off their thrones. Mu watched them sink, swirling around and around mem until their limbs no longer flailed. The water calmed and the Experienced bobbed on its surface like pine cones.

"I will not ask again Ayana."

Ayana blinked and the stench of burning hunmir returned. Mu stared at Takanori and the water in the basin stopped bubbling.

Takanori stood up and glared down at the carrier in mir chamber. "Will you continue to fulfil your island duty?"

Ayana rose from mir knees. Mir eyes again swept the Experienced but this time mu made sure to look at each of them directly. Ayana landed on Takanori and stared at mem long enough for mem to shift mir weight in discomfort.

"Yes," Ayana said through gritted teeth.

The Experienced exchanged glances and began to nod.

"You may return to the island," Takanori said, and with a flick of mir wrist gestured for Ayana to leave.

The wooden door creaked open and Ayana emerged, blinking, into the sunlight. Sana scrambled up from the patch of grass mu had been waiting on. Mu peered over Ayana's shoulder and was relieved to see Ayana was without escort.

"You are free to return to the island," Sana said.

Ayana nodded. "Will I see you again?"

Sana grimaced. "I hope not."

They looked at each other for a moment then Ayana fell into Sana's arms and they held each other for a while.

"I'm sorry but I have to leave now. I am sure Reo will

be eager to see you," Sana said, mir voice cracking a little.

Ayana lowered mir eyes to the ground. "I … I am glad it was you in the hut."

Sana smiled sadly. "In that sense, I wish I had never met you."

Tears prickled Ayana's eyes and mu quickly wiped them away.

"Goodbye, Ayana," Sana said, giving Ayana's palm a final squeeze.

"Goodbye Sana," Ayana said. But before Sana could walk away mu called out, "One last thing. Where can I find the nimi root?"

NINETEEN

Ayana

May - Orbit Ten

Kairi remained stuck to the floor despite the detail of Ayana's agony swirling through his mind. The only indication that he had heard anything was the dilation of his pupils.

"After leaving Sana I went straight to Reo. I still hadn't decided what I was going to tell him, but as soon as I looked into his eyes the truth escaped my mouth. He was devastated. And furious. But what could we do? Our maymus were gone. Not lost to the island. Destroyed. We still had to go to the creation hut. I knew the Experienced would be watching closely to see if I was trying to fulfil my island duty. I chewed nimi root every rise and didn't stop until tales of ankhs swirled around the island," Ayana scoffs and shakes her head. "It feels so foolish now, but there was a time when I thought the ankh movement would lead somewhere. Some Maymuans were whispering that twins alive on Mu proved that another way of living was possible. Maybe even without the Experienced. They pinned their hope on Kaori. They believed she could be the way. I stopped chewing the nimi and dreamed of a time when I could keep my maymus. When I felt your volcano rip Mu apart, I knew that time had come."

A knock on the door startles Ayana.

"What is it?" she hisses through the wood.

"We still can't find Kentaro," Miki answers.

"Keep looking," Ayana says, her head resting on the door, listening to the sound of Miki returning to her search for Kairi's only love.

Ayana glances down at Kairi. "Kentaro will not outwit Miki. She will find him. She is capable of more than you can possibly know."

TWENTY

Ayana

Mu – Fourteen orbits ago

Less than one moon cycle after recovering from mir ordeal in the carrier hut, Ayana returned to where Hana and Rui had been taken from mem. Mu was on the hunt for death. A scream pierced the dark forest. Ayana's heart thumped in recognition of the sound of an emerging maymu. Mu peered through the leaves and watched the rearers surround the carrier. Ayana grimaced. At least they would be distracted for a while. Mu tightened mir grip on the stingray spine in mir fist, its sharp tip glinting in the moonlight. Ayana trekked past the rearer clearing, forcing mir way through the thick forest until mu found what mu was looking for. A wooden hut with a door. Only the Experienced were allowed doors so this hut was surely a storehouse of secrets.

Ayana kicked the door opened and Miki jumped from mir stool in panic.

"Where is the other?" Ayana demanded.

Miki looked from the anguish in Ayana's face to the glint of the stingray spine. "Mu is not here."

Ayana's eyes swept the hut. It was a simple one room space with two stools, a tiny fire pit, and two blankets rolled up on the floor. Naho was not here.

Ayana growled in frustration.

"Are you going to kill me?" Miki asked.

"Yes," Ayana said, unnerved by how calmly Miki had asked.

"Why?"

Ayana scowled and spat, "Because you took my maymus."

Miki sighed, "Yes I did, Ay Ay."

The stingray spine clattered to the floor. Ay Ay? The hut floor had trembled when Miki uttered that oddly familiar name. Ayana scrambled to retrieve mir weapon. Mu jabbed the tip at Miki who watched mem without moving.

"Sit down," Miki said gesturing to the spare stool.

"Did you hear what I said? I am here to kill you," Ayana spluttered.

Miki nodded, "But first you will hear all I have to tell you."

Is this a trick? Ayana thought. Many believed that Miki was a demon in a Maymuan shell. But mu found memself stumbling to the stool and sitting down on it.

Miki dragged mir own stool over and sat down in front of Ayana.

"You can put that down. I won't fight you."

Ayana shook mir head, clutching the spine tighter. "Say what you have to say."

Miki stared at Ayana and said, "Rui is no longer alive on Mu."

Ayana lurched forward to stab Miki but, despite mir many orbits, Miki easily caught Ayana's arm and said urgently, "But Hana is alive. Listen, Ay Ay! You must listen!"

At the mention of mir maymu, Hana, Ayana's grip slackened and Miki seized the spine. Ayana waited for Miki's attack but it did not come. Instead Miki rose and shoved the tip into the ground in front of the door.

"I am not going to hurt you. At least not physically. You can take this when you leave."

Miki sat back down in front of Ayana.

"Where is Hana?"

"I will tell you but first you need to understand," Miki said.

"I don't need to understand anything! Where is Hana?" Ayana shouted.

"There is a prophecy," Miki said, ignoring Ayana for now. "I don't know the details of every glyph, but I know enough to be able to tell you that it says the twin who can carry will be cursed with the power to harness water and the twin who cannot will be cursed with the power to manipulate fire."

Ayana stared at Miki. *What is this ratty demon talking about? And what does it have to do with Rui and Hana?*

"The Experienced fear the fire. The fire twin can never live on Mu," Miki said with a deep frown. "There was a time, before Takanori, when both shells would be shattered, but now we are able to spare the carrier twin because Takanori has always underestimated the magnificence of water."

"Who is *we*?" Ayana asked, mir head aching from all mu had heard.

"Naho."

"And what if the twins are both carriers?"

"Then they both shall live," Miki said simply.

"And if they are not?"

Miki's face darkened, "Then they both shall die."

Ayana exhaled and shook mir head, trying to digest this horror.

"So Hana is alive?" It seemed so unlikely. Never, even in mir wildest fantasies of how to avenge mir precious maymu, had mu considered that either could still be on Mu.

Miki nodded. "And, Ay Ay, the sparing of the water twin is also the reason you are still alive."

Ayana closed mir eyes and allowed the collapse of the floor to swallow mir shell. Mu hurtled down deep into the fiery centre of the island. The truth scorched mir skin. Mu clawed mir way back up onto the surface and saw memself, mir palms plunged into still water, circles rippling from mir wrist. The water swirling and frothing.

"Ay Ay," Ayana repeated. Overwhelming memories began to flood and pool in mir mind.

For the first time, Miki smiled. "Yes. Ay Ay. You are a water twin. At birth we took you and raised you away from the rearers. And when the time came you entered the temple as an unnamed. As will Hana."

Ayana wiped tears from mir cheeks. "What happened to my twin?"

"You know what happened," Miki said firmly. "I delivered mem to the sky. I don't extinguish them. I am not a rearer."

"So it is the rearers who slaughter the maymus?" Ayana hissed.

"Now it is. In the past it was the duty of the Experienced," Miki said, and bowed mir head. "I am sorry I can only save one but it is better than none. And I have accepted that those I have not saved will be waiting for me in the eternal."

Ayana frowned and rubbed mir temples. "But the twins Kairi and Kaori live?"

"Yes," Miki said. "This I do not understand. They are the only twins ever to survive on Mu. Takanori must have plans for them. Maybe there is something in the prophesy that tells of those two surviving."

"It doesn't make sense. Why kill all who came before and after them?"

Miki held mir hands up in surrender. "I don't know, Ay Ay."

"I have heard many Maymuans whisper that Kaori has tremendous power over water and they say Kairi burns both inside and out," Ayana said, wide-eyed.

"Yes. Naho watches them closely. Kairi has a wild temperament. I can't believe Takanori has not snuffed it out. Why does mu not fear mem and the disruption?" Miki asked, almost to memself. "Anyway," Miki said, changing the subject abruptly, "do you still wish to kill me?"

Ayana had been staring at the floor, lost in mir own thoughts. Mu looked up at Miki in surprise. "No, of course not."

Miki gave a curt nod, "Do you want to see Hana?"

Miki and Ayana entered the ocean with a splash. The sun was not yet ready to rise. The cool sea water chilled Ayana's skin. Mu paddled after Miki who led mem around the island. They passed tangles of impenetrable habim and gnarled benme trunks. Eventually the jungle thinned and a small cove appeared.

Ayana squeezed the sea from mir braids and stared at the figure emerging from a cave in the white cliff.

Naho ran towards Ayana with mir arms outstretched. Ayana hesitated but mir feet lurched forward and mu fell into Naho's arms.

"Ay Ay," Naho murmured. "I can't believe you are here."

"Is mu still asleep?" Miki asked.

Naho reluctantly let go of Ayana and nodded. Gently holding mir finger to mir lips for silence, with mir other hand Naho beckoned for Ayana to follow mem into the cave.

On the floor lay five snoring maymus. Ayana gasped. Mu had been expecting to find only Hana in the cave.

"There are at least two twins born per orbit," Miki whispered.

Ayana looked closer at the maymus and saw that they were different orbits. Ayana stared at the smallest, loosely wrapped in gobu. Mu had beautiful dark skin, hair as tight and curly as Ayana's own, long eyelashes resting on a plump cheek, and a sweet nose and mouth gently inhaling then exhaling dreams. Hana's hand was scrunched up in a fist above mir head. Ayana leaned over and stroked from the tip of Hana's thumb to mir palm. Miki made to intervene but Naho held mem back. Hana's fingers fluttered open and caught Ayana's finger. Mu continued to snore softly. Ayana carefully lay down beside her maymu and wept quietly, mir finger snug in Hana's palm.

When the sun began to creep into the cave, Ayana peeled memself from Hana. Outside the cave, Miki and Naho were waiting.

"Can I visit mem again?" Ayana asked, mir voice shaking because mu already knew the answer.

"No," Miki said. "If what we do here was ever discovered, we would be unable to ever save a water twin."

"But what can I do?" Ayana wailed.

Inside the cave, the maymus stirred. Naho embraced Ayana again then disappeared back into the cave.

Miki led Ayana to the shore and looked over mir shoulder to check that Naho had gone.

"Ay Ay, you must develop your water skills."

Ayana scoffed, "What good will that do?"

"I am not a prophet but there are times I see what

others cannot. I have seen a flame. A flame that can only be extinguished by a fearless wave. There will come a time when we need your power."

"Who will?"

"I will. You will. Be prepared. That is what you can do now for your maymu. And for us all."

"There is so much I still don't understand," Ayana said, rubbing mir aching forehead.

Miki nodded in understanding. The magnitude of all Ayana had seen and heard needed to be digested. "In time you will. For now you must master your gift."

others cannot. I have seen a flame, Ayana, that can only be extinguished by a tumultuous wave. Someday, you will [illegible] the wind [illegible] your power.'

'It will [illegible] be prepared. That is what you can [illegible] for your journey [illegible] us all.'

'There's so much I still don't understand,' Ayana said, [illegible] her head.

'[illegible] in understanding. The [illegible] Ayana [illegible] and [illegible] to be directed. [illegible] you will [illegible] yourself.'

TWENTY-ONE

Ayana

May - Orbit Ten

Ayana leered over Kairi. Memories of Rui's slaughter had made her as bitter as Mu ganba.

"So you see? You are not special at all," Ayana spat. "You were never the first twin and it seems that in ripping apart Mu, you did exactly what Takanori wanted you to do. You used to sneer at carriers for giving away our power, but look what you did! You gave him your fire and in the end you torched yourself."

Kairi stared at Ayana, his eyelids blinking rapidly.

"I did as Miki instructed. Discovering I was a water twin changed everything. I was never as powerful as Kaori but I could feel water flowing beneath my skin, not just over my palms. Right here, three orbits ago, in your river, I started to teach Hana too, but I never told her why."

~

"Try again," Ayana said softly, watching the leaf sail down the river.

"I don't want to," Hana said, pouting.

"Don't pull that face at me!" Ayana said, and tapped Hana's lips with her finger.

They both laughed.

"Why do I have to do this?" Hana asked, peering into Ayana's face.

Ayana sighed and looked at her long-limbed maymu. If they were on Mu it would only be a few more orbits and Hana would be expected to create. "Because it's important." Hana looked distinctly unimpressed so Ayana continued. "I know you can feel it, Hana. The chill under your skin. The gurgle through your veins." Ayana gazed across the river to the opposite bank. "The rush of exhilaration as you enter the eternal flow."

"I don't feel like that," Hana said with a scowl, a little afraid of what Ayana had just described.

"Don't worry. You will. Go and pluck another leaf."

Hana skipped away, grateful for an excuse to escape the intensity for a moment. Ayana watched her flee through the reeds. She thought to herself, *how can I make*

Hana understand how vital it is that she masters her power but without revealing the source of her power? Across the stream the reeds on the opposite bank rustled.

"Here you are," Hana said, handing over a fresh leaf and plopping herself down beside Ayana.

"Watch." Ayana crawled forward and placed the leaf on the river then sat back on her heels. The current began to drag the leaf downstream. Ayana closed her eyes and her head began to bob gently from side to side. The leaf froze. Hana's head swivelled from Ayana to the leaf and back. Ayana exhaled and the leaf began to cross the river in a line as straight as a horizon.

"How come you can do it without putting your hands in the water? It's not fair," Hana whined.

Ayana's eyes clicked open. "Because I practised and never gave up."

The leaf sailed faster and with a splash leaped out of the river on the crest of a little wave and landed neatly on the opposite bank.

"Please return it, Kao!" Ayana shouted. A little face appeared between the reeds. "It's okay. You can come out."

Kao shyly stepped out onto the bank and picked up the leaf. She entered the water and paddled across to Ayana and Hana.

"That is amazing," Kao said, her eyes shining with wonder.

"See?" Ayana said to Hana,."You should be more grateful that I am teaching you."

Hana bowed her head at the reprimand, "I'm sorry."

Kao continued twirling the leaf in awe.

"Is Kai nearby?" Ayana asked.

Kao shook her head. "He is in the temple."

Ayana smiled. "Would you like to meet us here when we practise sailing the leaf?"

Kao nodded.

"But you must promise never to tell anyone. Not even Kai, Kairi, or Sana."

"I promise," Kao said earnestly.

"Good." Ayana took the leaf from Kao. "Now, Hana, kneel down and this time concentrate on the sensation in your shell, not the motion of the leaf."

Memories beside the river make Ayana feel even more confined in the temple cell. She looks at Kairi. Even if Miki can't find Kentaro, they must sacrifice Kairi. The Mayans have been whipped up into a frenzy.

"Are you hoping your Mayans will save you? Or have you already worked out what will happen next?"

Kairi blinks.

"As soon as your shell shatters, the rain will return. Your Mayans will rejoice and you can take some comfort in their gratitude for your sacrifice. Foolish Mayans! They are Maymuans after all; they won't recognise the truth. It will not be the gods who have made the rain fall. It will be me."

Ayana paces in slow circles around Kairi's shell. His eyes follow her every step.

"I found the other water twins. It wasn't difficult. Most had been assigned water hunter duty before becoming carriers. After Miki revealed herself to them, they were willing to join us on May. I thought a lot about Kaori and the monsoon she caused before I joined May. If she could make the rain fall for days, I wondered whether the opposite be achieved. Could we stop the rain from falling?"

Ayana finishes pacing and stands over Kairi. She tugs at her lank hair.

"It has almost killed me. It is much harder to cease the flow than to bring it on, but it is worth it. Kai will rule this land and you and May and Maymuans like Takanori will finally be over."

Ayana crouches over Kairi and strokes his cheek,

"I would feel pity for you if it weren't for Sana."

It was only six moons ago that Ayana had sat waiting for Sana on the banks of the ruined river running through

May. The reeds swayed in the cool breeze of the rise, their tips illuminated by the ascending sun. The last of the river whispered. Water trickled past Ayana, sweeping wisdom downstream.

Sana sat down next to Ayana and rested her head on her shoulder. Ayana strained to hear the river she had destroyed, desperate for an alternative to present itself. The river was silent. It had no solution to Mayan-made problems.

"It's okay," Sana said eventually. "We both knew this time would come."

Ayana, still staring across the cracked riverbed, began to cry.

"I have prepared a strong draught of kaka root, so if you are able to give me a moment to swallow it you can perform the usual ritual," Sana said, lifting her head from Ayana's shoulder. "Please don't cry. I am ready to die. I know Kao will be safe. Do you know she still, after all these orbits, has never mentioned that she comes here with you and Hana?"

Ayana grimaced and Sana took a moment to wipe the tears from Ayana's cheeks.

"I love you, Ayana. I have loved you since the rearer hut."

"I know," Ayana said, and cupped Sana's face gently in her palms. "And I love you."

Ayana pulled Sana's mouth to hers and they kissed.

"I am sorry I could not love you the way I loved Reo," Ayana said.

Sana leaned in and kissed Ayana again.

"You loved me more than enough."

Ayana's tears splash onto Kairi's cheeks.

"You destroyed so many beautiful shells. You deserve to die alone without love to guide you into the next.

A key rattles in the lock and the wooden door swings open. Miki looks from hysterical Ayana to incapacitated Kairi.

"We can't find him and it is getting pretty wild out there."

Ayana quickly wipes her eyes with the back of her hand. "Forget Kentaro. I will prepare Kairi now."

“I am sorry I could not give you the world I [illegible]
Kat.” Ayana [illegible]
[illegible] and [illegible] Ayana again.
“You [illegible] more [illegible]?”

Ayana's tears splash onto Kat's cheeks.
“You destroyed so many beautiful shells. You deserve to die alone without love [illegible] you into the next [illegible]”
A key rattles in the lock and the [illegible] door [illegible] open. [illegible] Ayana [illegible] Kat.
“We can't [illegible] and [illegible] here.”
Ayana quickly wipes her eyes with the back of her hand. [illegible] will [illegible] now.

TWENTY-TWO

Kairi

May - Orbit Ten

My legs writhe and thrash. I must join Kentaro. I can't let this wicked she be my end. I roll onto my stomach and bend into a crawl. With a leap, I escape through the open door.

Except I can't. The draught Ayana has given me has bound me to the dirty floor more effectively than any rope could. I hear her tears splash into the half coco shell she has filled with my nemesis: water. A stick rhythmically taps the inside of the coco as she stirs in dried indigo powder.

My heart aches for Ken-kun. I should have listened. *You recognised Ayana's true intent from the beginning.* I will my fingers to move, even a little so my urge to snatch the coco and smash in Ayana's face can be fulfilled. Nothing.

The only sensation I have is of my eyelids closing. Not really a sensation – just momentary flashes of darkness; blinks counting the time I have left in my shell.

Ayana approaches and dips her fingers in the coco and begins smearing blue dye across my chest. My heart pounds. I can't bear to look at her face. How could I have been so blind? I close my eyes. Anything to try and stop the fury pulsing through my mind. My breath becomes ragged. I could die here. Alone. Underneath my temple. Like a cockroach squished under a foot.

Never.

Breathe.

I must be seen. I must be remembered. She said so herself. When the rain comes it is I who will be thanked. Honoured. Immortalised.

I need to calm myself. Kai's face appears under my eyelids. Her betrayal doesn't change my Kai. He will lead. He will be my legacy. And of only one thing I can be certain; Ayana's depravity does not seep to the depths of slaughtering the mayus. Kai, Hana, Haru, and Riku will live. And in this thought I can finally find some peace. My breath calms.

The lock rattles for a final time.

"Prepare yourself for the ceremony," Miki says to Ayana. I hear her run through the open door.

Miki leans over me and stares into my face. She sighs and carefully drips liquid into my eye. I squeeze my eye shut but it is too late; my vision blurs and more drops are poured into my other eye. These shes are taking everything from me. My reality, my movement, and now my sight. I will leave my shell unable to see the land I created. Panic returns. My breaths compete to flee my throat and I am certain to choke right here.

"Breathe, Kairi," Miki says. "And open your eyes."

My eyelids blink rapidly and slowly Miki comes back into focus.

"It is a draught to ensure you feel no pain. You are running out of time. Through the eye is the fastest way," Miki explains.

My heart continues to pound, but I am able to breathe again.

Miki leans over to whisper in my ear, "You have much to regret in the next but I know Naho would wish you no pain here at your end. Seek her. And let her guide you."

I feel a pain not of the shell upon hearing Naho's name. *Will she be there? Or will he be waiting?*

"Kairi is ready!" Miki yells, and a patter of feet enters the cell. I am lifted onto the shoulders of strong Mayans. I stare up at the dark ceiling of the short corridor. I have no other prayer. *Namu May Mu*. The Mayans carrying me begin to jog and we burst out into a sun-soaked clearing. A roar erupts from the assembled Mayans. The crowd surges and Miki screams and lashes out at those who approach. We finally reach the base of the temple and begin to ascend the stairs.

The sun burns my upturned face. I think of those who have ascended before me: Goro, Kin, Sana. At the top I am lowered and carried towards the sacrificial table. I search for the mayus but they are nowhere to be seen. Perhaps that is a mercy. Instead I am surrounded by she leaders. How could I have been so stupid? Of course this was Ayana's plan all along. She penetrated my mind without any physical contact, by asking for permission to name Kai after me; by moving into the temple. Always there at every meeting, in every conversation; biding her time like a Mu nabgar. Those ratty flaming flowers. I should have drowned her then. I should have shoved her face in the river. And Miki's.

My back is laid down against the stone. The sun no longer shines on my face. It has been blocked by a huge, rumbling, black cloud. Ayana was speaking the truth. Soon the rain will fall.

I long for the sensation of water on my flesh; to plunge into the river, swarmed by burning flowers. The lost fire twins.

I am not the first. The eternal fire. The true May. But I was chosen. I am Takanori's creation. Why? What is this prophecy Miki was unable to explain to Ayana? Secrets. Always secrets with Takanori. And our carrier, Naho. Concealed places. Like that ankh on Naho's hand.

If I could sit bolt upright I would. The ankh! The one in the snake cave on Mu with Kaori. Something sparkles above me. For a moment I can see the mother of pearl ankh inlaid in the rock above the opening before me. But it is not. It is Ayana in her ceremonial robe, shimmering in the blades of sun desperate to pierce through the clouds.

I close my eyes. It doesn't matter. None of it matters. Mu has gone. I destroyed her and all her wickedness. Oh yes, she was wicked. And now these Mayans. My Mayans will enjoy a new land. A land I gave them. Ruled by my Kai.

I open my eyes and Ayana has a dagger held high above my neck,

"Mayan gods of land, sea, and air. Listen to our prayer. Our supreme leader's blood will drain. We beg you. Return our rain."

A clap of thunder rumbles the sky overhead. Ayana thrusts the knife down deep into my throat. The she leaders groan. A flash of lightning cracks. Silver veins crackle through the black cloud and it finally splits. Rain splashes on my head and I plunge into the eternal dark.

TWENTY-THREE

Kairi

Ku - Orbit Zero

"Kairi?"

A familiar voice. It is Naho. This place is bright but I can barely see her. Naho is surrounded by tiny black shadows. They swirl gracefully around her. I am drawn to her despite my fear. I approach and realise the shadows have form: tiny scrunched up fists; wrinkled little feet. They are hes.

I hesitate.

"You can pass through them. They are my burden not yours," Naho says. "They are the ones I did not save."

I walk through the shadow of the lost fire twins. Naho opens her arms wide and I fall into them.

"I love you." The love glyph warms… I want to say *warms my shell* but I am not sure I have a shell any longer.

I can see Naho as she was on Mu. I can feel her embrace so we both have some kind of form but I know we have changed.

"What am I?" I ask.

"You are you," Naho replies with a smile.

I wait for my anger but it does not come. Anger in this place does not feel right.

"Where am I?"

"We are in Ku."

"Ku?" I ask.

"We are in non existence."

I don't understand.

Naho strokes my face. "I am here to guide you. Before your rebirth you must restore yourself." She sighs. "In this time you became lost."

I feel fear again.

"When in shell we are at the mercy of the universe. But we have a choice; to either become a partner of the universe or remain a victim. There are even those who transcend partnership and become shapers of the universe."

The weight of what Naho is saying feels like it is too much to bear.

"You and Kaori had an extremely difficult experience in this time. I am sorry you remained a victim."

I fall into Naho's chest again and she holds me tight and whispers, "I was also a victim in my time."

We hold each other, the fire twins swirling around us both.

"There was a prophesy," Naho says. "It predicted the birth of twins, one born of water and one born of fire. Long before you and I existed it was decided no twins could ever live on Mu. By Takanori's time, the water twin could survive but the fire twin was slaughtered."

"Where is Takanori?" I ask.

For the first time in this place, Naho scowls. "Why?"

"Why?" I ask in disbelief. "Because I would like to know why I survived. It must have been because of Takanori."

"It was his decision," Naho answers carefully.

"So where is he?" I peer through the fleshy shadows, expecting him to appear.

"You will not find him here. This place is love. Takanori was incapable of love."

"Will I ever see him again?" I ask, afraid of the answer.

Naho shrugs. "I don't know. You may be reborn with him but you will not greet him here."

I wait again for an anger which does not come. I feel I want to cry but tears do not flow either.

"I am here to guide you, Kairi. In love. You must let go of Takanori. He is the antithesis of love. You have entwined yourself with him. Let him go or you can never be free."

I ponder what she is saying. "But where is he?"

"We no longer share a time. You must focus on restoring yourself."

My thoughts are scaring me. Words pour from within. "Are you saying that Takanori is lost? Then how can I possibly be restored? I shared so many terrible things with Takanori."

"You are not Takanori," Naho says firmly.

"But Miki said—"

"Miki talks too much," Naho snaps. I ignore her; the fear is too great.

"She said that we are all born with a star and mine was lost."

Naho inhales deeply. "Miki has immense knowledge of her time. And she was right. We are all born with a star but she should never have implied yours was lost."

Fear's stranglehold loosens a little.

"When in shell we all have desires. Our desires determine who we become. The glyph for desire means to be without star. The universe challenges us all to find our star. Eventually we are to realise it was always within."

The truth draws me further into Ku. I feel a greater detachment from my shell.

"Kairi, my love. You never found your star. You had no guide. You focused on what you hated not what you loved."

Panic swarms. "I need to go back. Please, Naho, send me back. I can do better next time." Naho gulps and my panic escalates. "What? Tell me. I will do anything. Just tell me what to do."

"You must wait."

"For what?'

"For whom." Naho says.

"Whom?" I ask.

Naho stares at me and I know. Kaori.

"And while you wait to help her pass, you must endure the shadows of those you slaughtered."

The faces of Goro, Kin, Sana, and Reo flash in front of me.

"In the waiting there is hope to find your star, in love." Naho watches me carefully.

What am I supposed to say? I guess the time for trying to find the easy way, the short cut, is over.

"Naho?" She looks at me with hope. "Am I capable?"

She rests her palms on my shoulders and her face shines with happiness. "Yes, Kairi, you are, because you are learning humility."

"But how do you know? How can I be sure I am even capable of love?"

Naho smiles wider and gently turns me around. "Look who also wanted to greet you."

A familiar little figure steps through the shadows. Her hair is a fuzzy black halo. It is the unnamed from Mu.

"I felt your love and pain from my passing," she says simply.

I don't know what to say. Heat burns inside – not the scorch of my flame, the lick of something purer igniting within.

"They are waiting for you," she says.

"Who is waiting?" I ask.

"Your shadows." She reaches her small hand out to mine. "Come on. I can wait with you for bit if you want."

I look at Naho. She nods. "Goodbye, my beautiful one."

"Thank you," I say. "For being here."

The unnamed tugs on my hand. "Do you want me to wait with you?"

I turn away from Naho and reach out to the unnamed.

"Yes please."

Hand in hand we step through Naho's shadows into mine.

Scroll Four

TWENTY-FOUR

Kaori

Blackland – Orbit Twelve

The air is heavy with death. Of all the herbs ground to embalm the shells, cloves come closest to masking the stench. But not quite. I resist the urge to squeeze my nostrils. The embalmers have paused in their duty and are watching me. When I first came here they were surprised, but now they only stop out of respect and wait patiently for my permission to resume embalming.

"Continue," I say.

In a cavern deep beneath the temple, three work the corpse. One inserts a hot rod deep into the nose, stirring until brain streams out. Another is neatly sewing up the incision made to remove the heart. The other is grinding fragrant pods, seeds, and petals in anticipation of preparing the skin. To one side are mounds of cloth which have been carefully torn into long strips. When the corpse is ready, it will be bound. Preserved. Not tossed in the air and ravaged by scavengers.

Now that the soft organs have been removed and the skin has been sewn together, they each dip their fingers into the embalming paste and begin massaging the dead flesh.

I approach the embalmer preparing the arms. The arms are as unblemished as my own.

"Another one?" I ask.

The embalmer nods.

I search the shell for the cause of death. The embalmer lifts the chin from its position of resting on the chest. The throat is slit.

An image of Aito hanging mutilated from a tree in Mu flashes before me. He never lived to see his son, Ren. I stumble. The embalmer grabs my elbow, accidentally smearing paste on my arm.

"Continue. Please continue," I whisper.

I stagger away from them, their stares burning the back of my neck. I try to calm my racing heart, but each breath brings the smear of embalming paste into my shell. Wiping my elbow with my hand only increases the scent. Blood rushes to my head and I hurry out of sight of the embalmers. Finally I spot a place to rest my head – an empty cell carved into stone. I place my palms flat and drop my face to the stone. The cloves from the paste on my hand fill the space. They are numbing. My heart slows. The snakelike vein that was pulsating in my neck rests. Tears spill and I bathe my face. Even this meagre amount of water is enough to soothe my soul. As always in these dark moments, I long for my carrier. Naho told me: *fear is responsibility; and honour*. I am afraid.

The shelf I am hiding in will soon be occupied by the freshly wrapped corpse. I can't rest here as though I too am dead. I pace slowly through the corpse chamber. The honeycomb cells are packed with Blacklander shells. In the most recently carved cells, the corpses are all unblemished. Someone is murdering all the Maymuans from my pod who never chose Kairi.

Since the slaughter of the ibis and the failed attempt to kill Saki, there has not been a public attack. Instead there is a steady flow of corpses piling up in here. Either slit throats or bulging eyes from suffocation. Some display the eternal sleep of the poisoned. The floor becomes a swelling wave. I rest my hand on a corpse-filled cell to try and steady not only my shell but my mind.

The rebellion was chaotic, frustrated and unorganised Blacklanders seizing their opportunity to riot. This is something else. It is methodical. Calculated. Terrifying. Blackland has become as claustrophobic as a forest beneath a looming thundercloud. The air is hot and oppressive on the skin. The urge to provoke is overwhelming. I long to rattle the cloud, to scrawl lightning across the sky, but I can't. It is not my cloud. I do not know what I would unleash.

It is the Kai. That much I know. But who are they? Where are they? These questions prickle my skin every rise. The unknown suffocates and overwhelms me. I have searched far and wide but still the unblemished die. The scarred loyal to me have tried to infiltrate the Kai yet not one has been brought to the temple and interrogated, never mind punished. A cold hand squeezes my throat. Are any of the scarred loyal to me? The only Blacklander I can trust is Saki. I want to trust Eri. I really do but often when I look at her I see the scarred baby her carrier was holding. Eri's loyalty to me is a betrayal to all she has known so I can't abandon her. I have to trust her. Now she has chosen the temple she can never return to her hut.

The cell in front of me has three people neatly piled up together. I stroke the bandages of the corpse on the top. It could be Ren, resting on me and Saki.

A sharp finger pokes my shoulder.

"Sorry, I didn't mean to frighten you," Eri says.

"How did you know I was here?"

Eri's eyes narrow a little. "Because you are always here." I don't know how to respond and thankfully she continues speaking. "It's Ren."

I feel afraid again. "Is he okay? What has happened."

Eri raises her palms in surrender to try and placate me. "Don't worry. It's nothing urgent but he is…" She searches for the correct glyph. "Unhappy in the garden."

I grunt in frustration and march along the corpse chamber, up the staircase, and return to the temple with Eri in my wake.

Ren is smashing clay vases with a rock and a catapult near the pond in the main garden. The guards stationed on the high surrounding brick wall watch him with their bows and arrows undrawn. I wish they would shoot at him, into the ground near his feet to shock him out of his tantrum. I could really do without this now.

"Thanks Eri. I can take it from here."

"Are you sure? I can wait, if you like," Eri says, her face sincere. I feel a stab of guilt for my doubts about her earlier. She loves Ren as if he is her own flesh.

"It's fine. I am sure he will come and find you soon enough." Eri smiles and re-enters the temple.

Ren is engrossed in his destruction and has not noticed my presence. He approaches the pond to retrieve his rock. The pond ripples and recedes a little. Ren peers in and spins around, searching for me. Our eyes lock and a wave from the pond crashes over him, soaking his tunic.

"Mumu!" Ren squeals with indignation.

The guards watching laugh. I give them a nod and they leave their posts and move out of earshot.

Ren shakes off the water like a jungle cat exiting a river. "You are so annoying."

I make a pointed glance at the shattered clay pots and Ren has the grace to blush.

"There are better ways to release tension," I say.

"Like what?" Ren pouts. "Maybe I should have thrown them at the wall."

"Come on," I say, and guide Ren to a tree trunk that has had a section hacked out and sanded into a long seating area, its orbit rings exposed and varnished. We sit together. I run my fingers over the gnarly bark at the back of the bench. It seems like only a few orbits ago when Ren would have eagerly curled up on my knee or at least lain down and rested his head on my lap. Now he is twelve orbits and he is leaning as far out of my reach as is possible without shunning me completely.

"What's wrong?" I ask.

"Nothing," Ren replies, kicking the back of his heels against the bark.

The garden is ablaze with red and oranges leaves. The pretty flowers abundant earlier in the orbit are resting. We are in a time to sow not reap. The heat is still oppressive and perfect for my favourite blooms at this time.

"Do you want a fig?" I ask.

"Whatever."

I pluck a couple of figs from the tree that is heavy with the sweet fruit. The scent is intoxicating and I resist the urge to bite straight into the flesh.

"Here you are." Ren accepts the fruit and bites into it as if it is honeycomb.

"Why do you always do that?" I snap. "How many times do I have to show you?" I pinch the base and split the skin open. Syrup runs down my wrist. I fold it inside out so the fleshy insides glisten. and offer it to Ren.

"I don't want it."

"Why not? Just try it this way. Then you won't get a sore tongue."

"I don't want it," Ren hisses.

"Suit yourself," I say and shove the fruit into my mouth. It is divine and I can almost enjoy it.

Ren throws his fig onto the ground. It rolls until his bitemark is facing up to the sun.

"I can't be here anymore."

I suppress the urge to sigh. "Where do you want to go?"

"Anywhere other than here!" Ren shouts.

"Okay," I say. "We could look into finding you an escort for a camel ride. You could explore the dunes."

"No."

I rub my tired eyes, forgetting about the fig juice on my fingers. Grateful for the reprieve from Ren's frustration, I hurry to the pond and rinse my hands. I dip the corner of my tunic in the water and use it to dab my eyes.

"Sorry about that," I mumble, returning to the log and sitting a little closer to Ren.

"Why can't I try and find Kairi?" Ren finally blurts out.

I am not surprised. This is a familiar conversation. As regular as a full moon but infinitely less serene.

"We don't know where he is," I say. It's true. I have no idea where my twin has landed or if he even survived the sea. I carry the bloodstone, always. It burns in my pocket now.

"So what happened after the tsunami?" Ren asks, for what feels like the infinite moon's time.

I can't restrain my sigh. "Kairi sailed away and we sailed in the opposite direction."

"But that means we need to go back to Mu and keep sailing until we get to Kairi," Ren says, oblivious to the insanity of his suggestion. "Takafumi says—"

"I have no interest in what Takafumi says," I snap, and Ren's mouth seals shut. "I'm sorry. I don't mean to hurt you but I can't listen to this anymore. If Takafumi insists on talking to you about Mu then the very least he could do is tell you the truth."

"What truth?" Ren asks eagerly.

Now my mouth seals shut.

"See? This is what I mean, Mumu. You don't tell me anything. At least Takafumi talks to me."

Yes. Talks a load of camel dung. Ratty Takafumi.

"Takafumi says," Ren continues, ignoring my teeth sucking, "that Kairi was the original he! Can you imagine? Being the original he?

"Who was the original she then?" I ask. Ren's face falls. "Oh, Takafumi hasn't bothered to tell you about shes. How unsurprising. He only talks about he."

"Well he is a he and so am I. Maybe that is why he only mentions he," Ren says, earnest in his explanation.

I feel an urge to smash something. "I would like to remind you that the three Blacklanders responsible for every breath you take on Blackland are all shes. What would you do without me, Saki, and Eri?"

Ren lowers his gaze and shuffles his toe in the dirt. "I know. But it is all so interesting." A spark ignites inside him again, "Is it true that Kairi can fire flames from the grass straight up to the moon?"

"Kairi was as gifted in fire as I am with water," I say through gritted teeth.

"Why can't I do anything with fire? I am so useless.

It's because of who you created me with, isn't it? I hear people talking. They say he was a coward."

"Now that's enough!" I roar and rise from the log. "You are never to speak about Aito that way. Do you hear me?"

"Yes," Ren says, staring down at his hands in his lap.

I sit back down, creating a distance between myself and Ren. I am going to kill Takafumi when I next see him.

"You have no idea what it was like on Mu," I say, unable to control my mouth.

"Then tell me," Ren pleads. "How am I supposed to understand?"

"There was a lot on Mu to be afraid of," I say, almost to myself. "The more I think about it, the more I believe Aito's response was normal. Yes, he was scared. We all were. But we all had our own ways of coping."

"What do you mean?"

"You asked about Kairi. He was afraid but he took his fear out on others. He used his fire to control and frighten us all."

"But he must have been so powerful," Ren says with an awe that churns my stomach.

"Yes, he was powerful, but fire without control is extremely dangerous. There are other powers. Respect. It is better to be respected than feared."

"Do you think the Blacklanders respect you?"

Ren's question strikes like lightning through my shell. "What do you think?"

Ren scoffs. "The ones with the scars definitely don't. Is it true you kidnapped them all? No wonder they don't like you."

I refuse to squabble with him. "You don't need to worry about Mu. Or Kairi. I sought out a new land so you never have to experience what we did."

Ren considers what I said and his fists clench. "I don't believe you thought of me at all! I think you just wanted to run away. Like stupid Aito. I wish I was with Kairi and not stuck here with you."

I don't bother trying to stop him when he runs off towards the temple.

Fireflies glow over the garden pond. The darkness has brought a chill, but I am not ready to return to the temple. The guards have not returned to their posts, wisely choosing to leave me alone with my misery. I have failed him. I raged across the ocean with the hope of a new beginnning but I haven't escaped Mu. Kairi's volcano threatens to erupt and destroy us again.

Why can't I be free of him? My fingers wrap around the bloodstone in my pocket. I stand up and throw it to the ground. My eyes scan the edge of the pond until I find what I am looking for.

Large rock in hand, I pound the bloodstone.

"I hate you. I ratty hate you!" I scream, whacking the bloodstone again and again. Sparks fly with each blow until finally it cracks. I roar up into the stars and they gaze down indifferently.

"Are you ratty happy now? You have my twin and now you have my son."

"Kaori?"

I spin around and Saki is there. Her white tunic shines bright like the breast of the ibis. I fall into her arms and she holds me tightly to her chest.

"Is Ren okay?" I ask when my sobbing finally subsides.

"Yes," Saki says, "He burst into our chamber shouting something about how you never tell him anything and treat him like a baby. Since then he has been in his own chamber. Eri took him some food and said he had calmed down."

"What the ratty hell is Eri doing? She is supposed to be watching him. How can I possibly attend meetings in the main chamber, supervise all the guards and workers, and rule ratty Blackland if I constantly have to worry about Ren?" I can feel hysteria brewing again.

"Why does he spend so much time with Takafumi? There must be someone else, anyone else he can talk to."

Saki sighs. "I understand." She strokes my face with her beautiful hand. "I mean that, Kaori. I know how difficult all this is for you and I am sorry it is happening."

I place my palm over hers. I love her so much. "Whenever I try and visit him during his tutor break he is never there."

Saki nods. "Eri says she also has tried to engage with him during the breaks but she always finds him in some corner of the temple whispering with Takafumi."

"Ratty Takafumi! I should have never allowed the Experienced to come to Blackland. I can't even get rid of them in death. After Takabe died I thought with them having so many more orbits than everyone else they wouldn't be around too long. But ratty hell, it seems like as soon as one dies they are immediately replaced with a rearer from Mu. Have you noticed? Who the ratty hell do they think they are?"

At times I can convince myself I have mastery over my anger but thoughts of anything from Mu quickly reveal I have as little control over my anger as I do over Ren.

Saki casts a furtive look around. "Do you think Takafumi has anything to do with the Kai?"

"I don't know," I say, my jaw clenching. "And if he does I can't prove it."

"It doesn't make any sense for the Kai to try and kill me and storm the temple but they haven't attacked any of the Experienced, who surely represent authority as much as you or I do."

"Unless the Kai don't consider the Experienced a threat because they are working together," I say, rubbing my aching forehead. "I have been in the tombs."

"Oh, Kaori. You need to stop it!"

"All right." I hold my hands up in surrender. "But listen, Saki, every new empty shell is from our pod."

"Really?" Saki gasps.

"Yes. I think the Kai are targeting my allies."

"But not the Experienced?"

"Or the rearers."

The fireflies have flown from the pond and the only light in the garden is from the moon.

"What did you mean earlier?" Saki asks.

"When?"

"You said something like 'You have my twin and son'. Who were you speaking to?"

A wave of embarrassment washes over me. "I don't know. I was upset."

"It was an interesting pairing. Kairi and Ren."

I ponder Saki's question. The moonlight bathes the garden in an eerie light, casting shadows. Spindly branches stretch like fingers clutching for fallen leaves just out of reach.

"I suppose I was thinking about he and she – or mu and may – when I was talking to Ren. I don't know. The way he was speaking about Kairi. It really disturbed me. It was like he was in awe of him."

"You have to remember it is all new and exciting to him. He doesn't really understand. He never knew Kairi, so he can create a perfect fantasy in his mind."

"But why does he want to? Are we not enough? And Eri. He loves Eri! Why is he longing for Kairi?"

"Ren only knows the split. He never experienced being whole."

Fire flares inside me, "Are you saying I am not whole because I wasn't a Maymuan?"

"None of us are Maymuans now, Kaori," Saki says, calmly refusing to reflect my anger. "We are all split. Ren is trying to find his way on Blackland. It is not surprising he wants to be with other men."

I stamp my foot, crunching the bloodstone further into the dirt. "It was better before. The worst thing Kairi ever did was tear apart mu and may. How will Ren ever know any peace as a man?"

"How will any of us? We are all condemned to live incomplete. There will never be peace until we are all able to embrace the he and she within us," Saki says with a frown. "That being said, I am not sure that Kairi was the first to split Mu."

"What do you mean?" I ask.

"I think the first split came when Takanori became obsessed with repopulating the island. He split carriers from everyone else."

The silence of the night is shattered by the clanging of bells. I seize hold of Saki. It is the bell to warn of imminent attack. Footsteps pound the high wall surrounding the garden as the guards resume their position, arrows drawn at what lies beyond the temple walls.

"We have to go," I say.

The bell abruptly stops clanging. A new peal rings telling us that the threat is over. A false alarm. I will have to find out who made such a horrible mistake. We can breathe again but the archers remain in position.

"We have to talk to Ren," Saki whispers.

"No."

"Kaori," Saki pleads, squeezing my arm tight.

"I said no." I shake off her grip. "He has not seen enough orbits."

"If he was on Mu he would already be paired and about to receive an island duty."

"Don't you see how wicked that all was? Look at Ren! He is so vulnerable and undeveloped. That is how we were, Saki! And look what the Experienced made us do." Tears sting my eyes and my throat feels as though I am being constricted by a Nile snake. "We were so innocent. We should never have been exposed to those terrible things on Mu."

Saki looks up at the archers stationed across the wall to defend the temple. I follow her gaze and my stomach churns. We are not safe. There are not enough bricks to build a wall high enough to protect Ren from all that is coming. I know better than most that when the river is in flow, it will find a way around any obstacle.

"I want to protect Ren as much as you do," Saki says, "but how much time do you honestly think we have left? It would be cruel to leave him so unprepared."

I stare into the tangled branches of the flowerless tree.

Sometimes we have to plant seeds we will never see grow.

being constrained by [illegible] walls. [illegible] present.
We should never have been exposed to those outside
things in Nail.'

[illegible] looks up at the architects scaffolded across the wall
to defend the temple [illegible] follow [illegible]
[illegible]. 'We are not safe. There are not enough [illegible] to
build a wall high enough to protect them from all that is
coming. [illegible] is better [illegible] when the [illegible] to
flee, it will find a way around any obstacle.'

'[illegible] as much as you do,' [illegible]
'but how much [illegible] do you [illegible] I [illegible]
[illegible] would [illegible] to leave [illegible] for [illegible] place?'

I stare into the tangled [illegible] of the [illegible] trees.
'Sometimes we have to [illegible] to see [illegible]
grow.'

TWENTY-FIVE

Kaori

Blackland – Orbit Thirteen

The clang of bells ricochets around the courtyard. Frightened shells rattle against each other in a desperate attempt to escape the confines of the temple. A swarm of invaders wrapped in black cloth advances, spilling across the desert like squid ink through water. The Kai.

I am desperate to flee with my people but I refuse to abandon the temple until I see the face of this threat. From the highest chamber in the temple, I lean over the balcony and watch the chaos below.

Guards stand shoulder to shoulder along the outer walls. The ink spill of invaders seeps within firing distance of the guards. A flurry of arrows flies into the invaders but they continue to advance. The guards load and fire again but still the Kai spill towards the gate.

"Defend the gate!" I scream, unheard.

Thankfully the guards have the same idea and they march from the walls to the gate.

Pound. The thick wooden gate trembles from the ferocity of the Kai.

Pound. Guards pile their shells against the gate. My tears fall to see the loyal Blacklanders join the guards in trying to defend our temple.

Crack. Even I hear the wood splinter from high up here.

"Run! Hide!" I scream.

The gate bursts open and the Kai enter the grounds of the temple. Arrows fly and guards and Blacklanders crumple to the floor.

"No!" I scream.

A sharp pain tears across my cheek. I touch the graze with my hand and my fingers are covered in blood. On the floor lies an arrow, the tip stained with my blood. The feathers in the shaft are iridescent black. The same feathers Ren received from Takafumi and the same feathers that protruded from the slaughtered ibis.

I peer over the balcony and a tall man with a shaved head is staring directly up at me. He, unlike the rest of the Kai, is not wrapped in black. He wears a black loin cloth as though he has jungle hunting duty on Mu; his quota Blacklander lives. His black skin is mottled from head to toe like Kairi's. I could fall into him I am so mesmerised by the sight of him. It is like Mu resurrected before my eyes. He smiles and with lightning speed draws his bow and shoots another arrow at my face.

I scream and duck in time to feel the sharpened tip graze the top of my head. Sickening groans and gasps of Blacklanders being slaughtered fill the courtyard. I crawl towards the door of the chamber. It swings open and Saki pulls me to my feet and we sprint down through the temple to our chamber.

Our chamber has not yet been infiltrated. Saki shoves some final items into a bag.

"I think this is everything you will need." Her voice trembles and I can't look at her. If I see her lovely face I won't have the courage to do what needs to be done.

"Are you absolutely certain Ren is safe?" I ask.

"Yes. He is with Eri as we agreed." Saki grimaces. "It is you they want."

I thought the carriers on Mu were so weak for giving away their maymus. How wrong I was. If they felt even a sliver of the anguish I feel now, I regret every judgemental thought I ever had about them.

Silence.

"The bells have stopped," Saki says. We both know this does not mean that the threat is over. It means it is imminent.

I scoop up the bag Saki has packed for me and head out of the chamber down the stone steps to our private garden that is lapped by the Nile. A small wooden boat bobs there. I toss the bag of supplies into it.

"Listen," Saki says her eyes wide. "They are coming. I didn't expect them to get here so fast."

Saki pulls me to her. Her hair, even in this terrible moment, smells sweet. I kiss her neck. I wish I could live inside her as Ren lived inside me. Safe, cocooned.

Saki screams and her shell crumples and slips through my arms. A black feathered arrow sticks out of her leg.

The man in the loin cloth stands at the top of the steps, arrow drawn ready to fire again.

"Don't hurt them! Please don't hurt them!"

Cold seawater floods my veins when I recognise the voice of my son.

Ren appears and pushes past the man. Eri appears and instead of seizing Ren she calmly lowers the man's bow.

"No Junta," Eri says. "Only Kaori. Leave Saki alone."

I look in horror from Saki to the boat.

"Go, Kaori. Please. Go," Saki murmurs, her voice weak from pain.

Junta fires another arrow and I roll towards the Nile. My hand reaches into the cool water and I launch a snake at Junta. It lands on his shoulders and plunges its fangs into his flesh. With a roar he pulls the snake out. The Nile splashes with snakes rushing from the water to attack. They slither up the steps; he tries to bat them away but there are too many. Their fangs pierce his exposed skin. He collapses and tumbles down the stairs with a crack of bone on each step. More of the Kai stream out of my chamber and freeze with shock at the sight of their fallen leader.

Saki's eyes are closed but mercifully her chest rises and falls with breath. Eri tugs on Ren's arm and tries to drag him away from the snakes and Junta's ruined shell. He looks to me for help, his eyes wide with terror. Every sinew in my shell longs to make everything okay for him, but I can't. Ren will never be safe as long as I am alive.

There is a scuffle on the stairs and Takafumi barges through the Kai. He sees me teetering on the edge of the river.

"What are you waiting for? Kill her!" he roars.

The snakes rush towards me. I lean back and with a splash I am swallowed by the Nile.

TWENTY-SIX

Takafumi

Blackland – Orbit Fourteen

"Namu Blackland," Takafumi says. Branches wrenched from fig trees in the garden crackle and snap in the fire pits.

"Namu Blackland," The assembled respond.

It could be the Experienced temple in Mu. Twelve wooden chairs are arranged in a half moon, occupied by the last surviving Experienced, Takako and Taketo, their leader, Takafumi, and a mix of rearers and members of the Kai. Unlike the thrones from Mu, the chairs are not woven into the floor. Instead, the backs of the chairs have been carefully carved to resemble a roaring fire. Iridescent black feathers flicker like flames across the top of the headrest.

The chair usually reserved for Ren is occupied by Eri.

Takafumi has made sure to seal the chamber so the boy cannot enter.

"We are gathered to discuss the fate of Ren," Takafumi says. The assembled squirm in their chairs and cast furtive looks at each other. "More than one Blacklander in this chamber has approached me to ask if the boy is necessary. Speak freely and let us resolve this issue."

The only sound to be heard is the torment of the burning branches in the firepits.

"I don't think we need him anymore," Takako finally bleats.

A murmur of agreement can be heard from some of the others but Taketo rolls his eyes,

"Why do you want to spoil what we already have? The Blacklanders love the boy. He is doing everything we want him to do. What is the problem?"

"I don't trust him." Takako scowls and some nod in agreement with her. "And stop calling him a boy. He's fourteen orbits now."

"That is not a good enough reason to kill him!" Taketo scoffs.

Takako glares at him and bends her index finger back, ready to reel off a list of Ren's transgressions. "He doesn't have the stomach for punishment. Have you ever seen him at any of the sacrifices or corrections? No. And that is the main reason the Blacklanders like him! He washes his hands of any violence and the Blacklanders hate the Kai who have to perform them."

"Yes!" the members of the Kai grunt.

"And"—Takako continues bending another finger to count Ren's failings—"he is attached to that ridiculous she, Saki. He barely leaves her side. It is pathetic. I don't understand why it is allowed! Why is Saki still breathing on Blackland? Surely we can all agree that she can never be trusted."

"But he loves her," Eri says simply.

"So what?" Takako snaps.

Eri gazes calmly at Takako. "So letting him be with Saki means he has never rebelled against anything we have asked him to do. He may not attend the trials but he has never interfered. I agree with Taketo. Why change something that is working so well?"

"Well, you would say that because you are as infatuated with him as that silly she Saki is," Takako sneers. "They share the same chamber every rise. No one knows what they discuss. It is dangerous."

"Enough!" Takafumi commands. "Eri has shown her loyalty. Are you suggesting otherwise?"

"No," Takako mumbles.

"Saki is not a threat. Eri watches them closely enough," Takafumi says.

"How can we be as sure as you both are?" Takako says.

"I'm sure," Taketo says with a smirk.

"Your opinion is not as valuable as Takafumi's," Takako snaps.

Takafumi sighs, tired of the last two surviving Experienced squabbling.

"What is it you want?" Eri asks.

"I want proof of his loyalty and commitment to Blackland," Takako says.

The Kai stand up from their chairs. "We wish for the same."

The chamber is split and Takafumi knows something must be done.

The firepits, extinguished after the secret meeting, had flooded the chamber with noxious smoke. Takafumi is grateful to gulp some fresh air in the garden. He strolls across the moonlit grass, his mind overflowing with Takako's demands. A rustle alerts him that someone else is here too. He peers around a bush and sees Ren sitting alone on a hollowed-out tree trunk. He watches as the boy carefully breaks open a fig, gently pushing the fleshy insides outwards. The boy closes his eyes and places the fig into his mouth, chewing and savouring every morsel.

Something in the boy's mannerisms and expression repulses Takafumi. Perhaps Takako is right. Maybe this boy is too weak for Blackland. A branch cracks under Takafumi's foot and Ren sits bolt upright and searches for the sound.

"Ren," Takafumi says, stepping out of the shadow.

Ren gazes up at Takafumi, his eyes wide and startled. In the moonlight, Ren's tight skin shines and Takafumi reflects on how few orbits the boy has lived. But Takako is right, on Mu he would be a hunter fulfilling his island duty, not sitting in a garden trapped like prey.

"We missed you at the last correction," Takafumi says.

Ren manages to control a shudder. Correction is such an inappropriate word for the punishments the Kai inflict on disobedient Blacklanders. Maiming would be the glyph Ren would use. A severed finger, foot, or sometimes even a tongue is the price of displeasing the Kai.

Takafumi stares at the boy. "I must insist you attend the next correction."

Ren blinks rapidly.

"I feel your Blacklanders should know you approve of the Kai rulings. We wouldn't want any kind of rift now, would we?"

Ren looks anywhere other than at Takafumi. The silent night waits for Ren's response.

"Okay. I will be there," he whispers.

Takafumi smiles and returns to the temple, leaving Ren alone beside the fig tree.

The first trial Ren attended he was too shocked to speak. He took his place on the centre chair next to Takafumi. The Blacklander was accused of stealing fishing rods from a boat anchored on the shore at low tide. The correction was a severed thumb and finger. Ren appeared ready to vomit but even Takako could not say the boy did not fulfil his duty.

Gradually Ren found his voice.

"What is the disobedience?" Takafumi asks.

The Blacklander thrashes and writhes between the tight grip of two members of the Kai.

"Nothing. I didn't do nothing," the Blacklander shouts.

"Stealing panels of wood from the temple," the Kai member reports.

"I thought they were scrap. I found them outside the gates. The roof of my hut leaks."

"Silence!" Takafumi booms. "One foot."

"No!" the Blacklander wails.

"Do you still have the panels?" Ren asks urgently.

The Blacklander and the Kai holding him look to Ren in surprise.

"Yes," the Blacklander says.

"Return them. Next," Ren says.

"But—" splutters the Kai.

"I said *next*," Ren commands. The other assembled rustle in their chairs, but what can they do? The chamber is full of Blacklanders who view Ren as the ultimate authority. This is not a secret meeting in which they can undermine him.

Takafumi bows in acquiescence and the Kai release the Blacklander. For a moment he staggers, unable to comprehend his freedom. He flees towards the chamber opening before his luck runs out. At the last moment, he turns and bows to Ren.

Takako glares at Takafumi and Takafumi knows he will receive a furious rant from Takako before the sun sets.

Ren is desperate to stretch out his limbs. He has been sitting on the chair since sunrise. The sun has begun to set but still the Kai drag in more Blacklanders to punish. Ren is used to Takako's eyerolls and audible teeth sucking by now. He doesn't care. As he has explained to her numerous times, it is inefficient to keep maiming Blacklanders then expect all of the Blackland duties to still be fulfilled. It is best to use minimum correction, then when a disobedience is severe enough the correction will have maximum impact.

Ren stifles a yawn. It was tiring listening to all of these petty transgressions and then moderating the Kai. He considers standing up and stretching his legs when the atmosphere in the chamber changes. The hum of chatter ends as abruptly as the flame of a torch dunked in water.

Eri approaches the assembled … dragging Saki.

Ren leaps from his chair.

"Sit down," Takafumi barks.

Ren's eyes sweep the faces of the assembled and he shudders when he sees Takako licking her lips.

Ren slumps in his chair. He longs for the power of Kairi to incinerate this chamber before whatever is about to happen happens. But he does not have the power of Kairi and instead all he can do is close his eyes and hope to wake in another place.

Takafumi clears his throat, the sound echoing across the silent chamber. "What is the disobedience?"

Saki shakes off Eri's tight grip and defiantly positions herself directly in front of Takafumi.

"Engaging in forbidden conversation and desecrating the temple," Eri reports, her voice trembling a little.

"I saw her," one of the Kai shouts from the opening. He runs towards the assembled, eager to snitch on Saki and seal her fate. "She was drawing ankhs in the sand

and trying to convince a Blacklander that Kaori will one day return."

Takafumi and Saki stare at each other. Without breaking his gaze, Saki uses her foot to scrawl an ankh into the dust on the floor.

"See! I wanted to bring her to you but she"—the Kai jabs a finger at Eri—"insisted on presenting her instead."

"Yes I did." Eri says, scrubbing the ankh away with her foot.

"There is only one correction for forbidden conversation," Takako shrieks. "No matter what the boy says."

Ren feels the floor beneath him shift. He clutches the armrests of the chair as the chamber begins to spin.

"The tongue," Takafumi booms.

Eri backs away and the Kai swoop on Saki. They force her to the floor face down. One holds her chin and forehead and another forces open her mouth.

"Wait!" Takako cackles. "Use the boy's dagger."

A member of the Kai marches towards Ren. The boy feels he has no choice but to hand it over. It is the shape of an ankh. The handle is mother of pearl and the blade lies in a snake skin sheath. It is Kaori's knife.

Ren raises his eyelids enough to see the flash of metal. The flash becomes a dizzying swarm of silver bees nudging him off his chair. He slumps to the floor to join Saki, her smeared ankh, and her severed tongue.

and trying to convince [illegible] that [illegible] one [illegible]

Jakafumi and [illegible] [illegible] [illegible] [illegible]. Without [illegible] her [illegible] [illegible] [illegible] [illegible] [illegible] into the dust of the floor.

"And I wanted [illegible] her [illegible] [illegible] [illegible]—the [illegible] [illegible] a finger at himself [illegible] presenting her instead."

"Yes I didn't [illegible] [illegible] grumbling the [illegible] [illegible] way [illegible] the [illegible].

There is only [illegible] [illegible] [illegible] [illegible] conversation," [illegible] [illegible] [illegible] [illegible] [illegible] the boy says.

Ren feels the floor beneath him shift. He notices the [illegible] of his chair as the chamber begins to spin.

"The singing," [illegible] [illegible].

[illegible] [illegible] [illegible] [illegible] [illegible] [illegible] on [illegible]. They [illegible] [illegible] to the floor [illegible] [illegible]. One [illegible] her chair, [illegible] [illegible] and [illegible] [illegible] open her mouth.

"Wait!" [illegible] [illegible]. [illegible] [illegible] [illegible] [illegible].

[illegible] [illegible] of the [illegible] [illegible] toward Ren. The boy [illegible] [illegible] [illegible] [illegible] to [illegible] [illegible] [illegible] the ship [illegible]. The handle is mother-of-pearl and the blade [illegible] [illegible] [illegible] [illegible] [illegible].

Ren raises his eyelids enough to see the flesh of [illegible] the [illegible] [illegible] [illegible] [illegible] [illegible] [illegible] [illegible] [illegible] him off his chair. He [illegible] to the floor [illegible] [illegible] [illegible] and [illegible] [illegible] [illegible] [illegible].

TWENTY-SEVEN

Takafumi

Blackland – Orbit Fifteen

Blue lotuses bob on the calm Nile. Takafumi watches from a raised platform as they traverse the lanterns illuminating the dark water. There had been a fear since Kaori's escape that the Nile would no longer flood, but Kaori had fundamentally changed the natural rhythm of the water. In the rises leading up to the bloom of the blue lotus, it was clear the Nile was ready to flood.

'No, she shouldn't have so much power,' Takafumi thinks to himself, gazing into the blur of blue petals and fire. He is extremely grateful the boy does not share Kaori or Kairi's abilities. He doesn't seem to have much to him at all considering who his carrier was. As much as Takafumi despised Kaori and everything she represented, he can't deny she had courage.

Ren sits beside Takafumi watching the procession of blue lotuses across the water. Saki stands as always by his side. Her maiming has removed her ability for speech but not her loyalty to Ren. Takafumi can't understand her behaviour. She was not his carrier. Why does she still care so much about the boy?

Saki's fingers squeeze the back of Ren's chair. A raft carrying an ibis sails the Nile. Since the attempt on Saki's life, the blue lotus ceremony had continued without crowds and without using an ibis. Kaori had refused to risk Saki's safety ever again by exposing her on the water.

This ibis is escorted by a member of the Kai. Takafumi has very different intentions for the ibis than Kaori had.

The water ripples as the raft sweeps across its surface.

"Kai!" the rower shouts, bringing the raft to a stop before the platform.

The spit of arrows fills the air. Ren and Takafumi stand and watch the arrows arch through the sky towards the proud white chest of the bird. The raft begins to tremble and long black slashes dart across the ibis's chest. Kaori's Nile snakes have tried to save the ibis. With a splash they return to the Nile impaled with an arrow from the Kai. The ibis's wings flutter. It is still alive.

The crowd of Blacklanders murmur in confusion,

unsure of how to react. They had been promised a sacrifice.

"Kill it!" Takafumi roars.

The rower reaches out to strangle the neck of the ibis but again snakes erupt from the Nile. They constrict him and he drops like a stone into the dark water.

The platform erupts in pandemonium.

"Someone kill it!" Takafumi shrieks.

Eri runs onto the platform wielding a bow and arrow. Ren snatches it from her, loads an arrow, and time seems to slow as the arrow arches toward the ibis. A piercing scream rattles the sky. The magnificent bird that was a poignant symbol of hope for Kaori slumps, Ren's arrow through its heart.

The crowd roars in approval.

"Well done!" Takafumi says, clapping Ren on the back.

Ren gives a tight smile in return. The crowd chant Ren's name.

"From now on," Ren tells Takafumi, "I will lead the temple corrections."

Saki, unable to speak, instead wipes tears from her eyes.

[illegible] power [illegible]. They [illegible] been [illegible] sacrifice.

"[illegible]," [illegible].

The [illegible] cut [illegible] of the [illegible] but again snakes [illegible] from the [illegible]. [illegible] and he [illegible] like a stone into the dark [illegible].

The [illegible] empties [illegible].

[illegible] shrieks.

[illegible] and arrow. Ken snatches it from [illegible] an arrow [illegible] seems [illegible] toward the [illegible] of the [illegible] sacrifice [illegible] poignant symbol [illegible]. Ken's arrow [illegible].

The crowd [illegible] approval.

'Well done,' Takatani says, clapping Ken on the back.

Ken gives a [illegible]. The crowd [illegible] Ken's [illegible].

'[illegible],' Ken tells [illegible] you [illegible] the [illegible].'

[illegible] unable to speak [illegible] tears from [illegible]

TWENTY-EIGHT

Takafumi

Blackland – Orbit Sixteen

The wind pulls the cloth tight over the face of a mysterious statue that is almost as tall as the temple. Unsurprisingly, given that Ren has loved cats since he could crawl, four paws have been carefully etched into limestone and the shell of a large feline rests beside the temple. Takafumi taps his foot against the balcony rail with impatience. What is the point of this grand unveiling? Ren demanded they build this monstrosity and now they have all gathered to finally reveal the face.

Since Ren took over the temple corrections, there haven't been any Blacklanders maimed. To Takafumi's surprise, rather than view the boy as weak the Blacklanders love Ren even more. His gentle corrections;

admonishments rather than violence; restoration instead of retribution. The Blacklanders idolise him.

The absence of violence rendered the remainder of the Kai obsolete. Some refused Takafumi's command to disband quietly, too attached as they were to the power of the temple. However, the vengeful maimed Blacklanders soon made sure to banish the hardcore Kai.

"Where is he?" Takafumi mutters and Takako and Taketo murmur their lack of an answer. The sun burns high in the sky, scorching the crowds of Blacklanders surrounding the statue.

Finally there is commotion within the chamber and Ren appears, resplendent in a bright white robe and wielding a long gold snake staff, flanked by Saki and Eri. The three remaining Experienced, rearers, and guards part to let Ren take his place on the balcony. The Blacklanders roar their approval at the sight of their leader. Takafumi grabs hold of Eri's wrist.

"What took you so long?" he hisses.

"Some final preparations," Eri says.

Takafumi stares at Eri. "Is there something you are not telling me?"

Eri gasps as Takafumi squeezes her arm painfully. "No," she says through gritted teeth. "Enjoy the ceremony."

Despite the scorching midday heat, Takafumi feels a chill. He looks to Saki who is standing next to Ren. She feels his gaze, turns, and smirks. Takafumi almost chokes trying to swallow his apprehension. It's surely only the heat and the waiting causing his unease, because what could the boy possibly do with a statue that could threaten Takafumi's position? With a sigh, Takafumi tries again to relax, but unease swirls through his shell like the sand blowing around the statue.

Ren raises his arms and addresses the crowd of Blacklanders.

"My dear Blacklanders, thank you for the many moons you have sacrificed to chisel and carve this magnificent monument." Ren pauses and Saki reaches out to gently rub his back. "This monument has been constructed to honour the original Blacklander. The one with the courage to seek a new land."

The Experienced rustle with confusion, searching each other's faces for an explanation. Takafumi marches towards Ren to drag him from the balcony, but before he can reach him a gasp erupts from the crowd below. Takafumi looks upon the unveiled face of the statue and finds Kaori peering down at him.

"Grab him!" Takafumi yelps, but no one moves. "Grab him, I said!"

Ren calmly turns to face the guards. They make no movement to seize him. Takafumi groans in frustration. He has spent his entire time on Blackland installing Ren as leader, plotting and planning. His wish is reality. The guards obey Ren.

"Take the Experienced to the meeting chamber and hold them there," Ren says. Takako thrashes against the guards but Taketo doesn't bother resisting. "Not you, Takafumi. You will stay here."

"Eri?" Takafumi implores. "What is this?"

Eri moves to stand next to Saki. With Kaori's face glistening in the sun behind them, they hold hands, united against Takafumi.

Takafumi's eyes dart around, searching for an escape. The gasp from the crowd of Blacklanders below has become a hum and buzz of excitement. What is the meaning of this statue with Kaori's face?

"I understand," Takafumi splutters, "the urge to see your carrier. It is admirable. But Ren, listen to me. Don't destroy all we have achieved here. You need me."

"I have never needed you," Ren spits. "Why would I depend on a man who underestimated the woman with the power to destroy an entire island within one rise? My mumu knew you would try and turn me against her. She knew everything!"

Saki and Eri nod in agreement with every glyph Ren utters. Takafumi trembles with rage.

"So what is the plan?" Takafumi snarls, and gestures to the chamber opening. "Is Kaori waiting outside? Does she expect to return? The Blacklanders will not accept her. They never respected her." Takafumi laughs; it is a wicked bark that grinds Saki's teeth together.

"Because of you," Eri snaps. "You have been plotting against Kaori ever since we all landed here! You didn't even try to hide it. Of course Kaori knew you were involved in the Kai. The arrow used to slay the ibis had the exact same black feathers as the one you gave to Ren."

Takafumi's eyes narrow. "What good did it do her to know? The Blacklanders love Ren but not enough for Kaori to return. You heard them when they saw her face. There were gasps not cheers. The Blacklanders may tolerate the boy's infatuation with his carrier but they will never again accept Kaori as leader."

Saki twitches beside Ren and Eri, desperate to interrupt Takafumi but unable to without her tongue, so his rant continues. "You have filled the boy's mind with tales of a brave leader. Kaori had no choice but to flood Mu. She was following Kairi. As she always did. If she knew I was in the Kai, why didn't she do something? I will tell you why. Because she is a coward. She ran away. She abandoned you all."

"No," Ren says, taking a step towards Takafumi. "My mumu is the bravest Blacklander ever to walk the dunes. She knew fear and she embraced it. She told me an incredible story. It was after your attack on Saki at the blue lotus ceremony. She went to flood the Nile, but when she was in the river she saw a small green fish lie still and let others feed on it. When a bigger fish appeared she told me she felt a fear unlike anything she had ever experienced in water. She panicked and fled but she couldn't stay away. She went back and saw the bigger fish was circling, biding its time, but when it finally made its move to strike, the green fish sprang to life. It was a trick! Other green fish appeared and trapped the big fish, eating it alive. Can you imagine the patience it took for the green fish to wait? To know another wished to destroy it, but instead of exhausting itself in battle it waited until the big fish thought it had won."

Ren, Saki, and Eri stand shoulder to shoulder watching Takafumi flail in Kaori's trap. Ren closes his eyes. The sound of the crowd beneath Kaori's statue fades away and he returns to the chamber four orbits ago when Kaori told him everything.

Kaori knelt down and gently stroked Ren's face. Saki peered around the door, checking the hallway one final time before closing it softly and joining Kaori to face Ren.

"Don't worry," Kaori said. "Eri is distracting Takafumi and we will hear footsteps if anyone else approaches."

"I know. Sorry – I can't help worrying," Saki said.

Ren looked from Kaori to Saki, his jaw clenched with anxiety. Saki reached for his hand and Kaori took a deep breath and began, "I am sorry, my love, but we are out of time. I had hoped to build a new land for you, a place of peace, but Takafumi will not rest until I am gone. He has assembled an army in Kairi's name – the Kai – and they intend to overthrow my rule and replace me with you."

"But I wouldn't do that! You know, don't you, mumu, I would never betray you," Ren said, his face flushing with passion.

"We know," Saki said. "But from this rise you must never let Takafumi believe he has anything other than your absolute devotion."

Ren's gaze dropped to the floor. "He says things…"

"I know what he says," Kaori said, lifting Ren's chin so she could look into his eyes. "And I know my son better than he ever will."

"I am scared," Ren said, finally admitting his true feelings.

Kaori smiled. "Good. It would be foolish not to feel fear at this time but we will always be with you – Saki, Eri, and I. No matter how it appears to Takafumi and the Kai, we will always be united."

Saki nodded. "Some terrible things may happen, Ren, to prove your loyalty to Takafumi."

Ren gulped and squeezed Kaori's hand.

"Isn't there another way?" Ren pleaded.

Kaori stroked Ren's hand in hers. "No."

"Soon Kaori will leave Blackland. It is the only way to ensure your safety and the future of Blackland."

"No!" Ren wailed. "I have been so horrible to you. Please don't go."

"You haven't been horrible to me. We are living in a difficult time. I love you and I know your strength. You will be an extraordinary leader of Blackland."

Silence filled the chamber as the reality of the situation rattled Ren.

"I don't know how to lead," Ren said.

"You will learn. First you must do as Saki says and make Takafumi believe you are following him and turning against me. Saki and Eri will guide you. Pretend to follow him with your actions but not your heart. Eventually he will allow you to lead. Protect the Blacklanders and you will have their loyalty. Then strike. Takafumi has to go."

"Will I have to kill him?" Ren whispered.

"No. Or the foundation of your reign will be built on violence. Once you use violence, it becomes impossible to rule without it. Banish him, and all the remaining Experienced, rearers, and the Kai. Split them up and send them to the far corners of Blackland. Their fate is their own."

"But then what?"

"Then you must decide how to rule," Saki said simply.

"I don't know how."

"It is your choice," Kaori said. "But a great evil was orchestrated by Kairi on Mu. I know this will be strange for you because you have never known anything other than the split. You must decide whether you want to continue being a he."

"How can it be a choice?" Ren asked.

"On Mu we used mu, mir, and mem for everyone instead of the split we have now. Saki and Eri will teach you more about the history of Mu, but for now I urge you to reunite the Blacklanders. No more he and she."

Ren's face was scrunched up in confusion, "But I thought living on Mu was horrible."

"It was," Kaori said, "because of Takanori. Without the fanaticism of the Experienced, mu, mir, and mem could work."

"We were never truly united," Saki explained. "Takanori was obsessed with populating the island so we were divided into those who could carry and those who could not. The carriers were always seen as weaker. Kairi knew this, and that is why he was so keen to split into he and she and secure the illegitimate power of he. Here in Blackland Kaori has tried to unite men and women but some wounds can't be healed."

"But what is wrong with being separate? Isn't there a way to remain as we are but succeed?" Ren asked.

Kaori considered his question. "I don't think so. It seems that when splits occur there immediately follows an assignment of value. Man becomes opposite to woman in every way. If he is strong then she must be weak. If he is born to lead then she is born to serve. It never ends. And it is destructive for both. We are balanced beings. He and she. May and mu. Unnatural splits weaken us all."

Ren sighed. "But what about creating?"

"You have spent enough time in the garden to understand the rhythm of life. When have the seeds failed to bloom? Let the Blacklanders create how and when they want. Trust. As long as you respect the balance within yourself and teach others to do the same, then you have nothing to fear. You will flow in the eternal river. Control your may impulse to consume and there will be enough to support all new life. Listen to your mu when it tells you to pause. Breathe, nourish, and heal."

"You will never be able to lead without me!" Takafumi snarls.

Ren's eyes click open, his precious mumu lost to him again.

"You are incapable of taking responsibility for them." Takafumi's arm sweeps out over the balcony, gesturing to the Blacklanders.

"I will give the Blacklanders the resources to provide for themselves," Ren says. "No more temple rule. All shall have the means to sustain themselves every moon and those who are unable, the temple will support. It is time to open the temple doors and let the Blacklanders in. I will serve them. They do not serve me."

"You are a fool!" Takafumi barks.

You, my love, can achieve what I never could.

Ren smiles, remembering the last glyphs his mumu spoke to him. He gestures to the waiting guards. "Take mem away."

"Mem? Oh, you truly are as stupid as your carrier," Takafumi scoffs, his mouth foaming with rage. "Don't you realise what you are giving up?"

"I know exactly what I am giving up. I have lived as a he, a man, and I am not ashamed of that, but the balance stolen by Kairi must be returned. Look at them!" Ren says, pointing at Eri and Saki. "You had no idea she was working against you! Saki gave her *tongue* for Blackland to keep you in the dark about my true loyalties. How could I dare believe myself to be above them? If I continue with he I will be living a lie. My power would be great but as fundamentally unstable as a sand dune. It is my honour to embrace my she as well as my he. Namu May Mu."

On the horizon, wind swirls the dunes. A storm of sand brews and approaches the temple. The guards drag Takafumi away, his fury unheard beneath the howl of the wind. Takafumi takes a final look at the monument Ren has created of Kaori, ensuring her legacy, and remembers the murmuring of the dying Blacklander.

"One will rise, and never be forgotten. The other will fall, betrayed by their own flesh."

Kaori, immortalised in Blackland, adored by Ren, Saki, and Eri; Kairi, on the path to self-destruction since leaving the Experienced temple on Mu.

The storm screeches across the desert.

"Here mu comes," Ren says, huddling closer with Saki and Eri.

Kaori roars over the balcony. Mu is a sandstorm, delirious in mir delight.

Kaori chases Takafumi out of the temple, blasting the doors off, leaving a vast opening for the Blacklanders to enter. Mu tears through the gardens, smashing down the walls dividing Blackland. Mu returns to the balcony and ruffles the hair of the three mu loved the most.

Kaori's force begins to weaken. It is time to rest.

In amongst the crowd of Blacklanders at the foot of the sphinx a stranger slumps to the floor in exhaustion.

Their emaciated shell is shrouded in cloth. Only their dark eyes are visible. They crawl their way through the tangle of legs and emerge blinking into the sunlight. The twinkle of the Nile calls the weary stranger to its banks. Finally surrounded by swaying reeds they can smell the Nile. Slowly they unwrap the cloth. Hair, matted with orbits of desert, tumbles onto a sunburnt collarbone. A stomach, swollen from lack of food, rests on a sharp hip bone. Feet, blistered from the wandering of an exile, are dipped into the Nile. Kaori sighs, it feels good to stop. The water ripples and black snakes rise to greet their master.

"I am ready." Kaori says. The sandstorm was Kaori's final act on Blackland.

The snakes wrap around Kaori's ankles and together they slip into the embrace of the Nile. Kaori is constricted and sharp fangs pierce flesh.

Kaori offers a final prayer to the sky above, "You did all I asked of you. Live well my love. I will see you in the next."

The water gurgles and Kaori's shell sinks beneath the surface.

TWENTY-NINE

Kaori

Ku - Orbit Zero

"Kaori?"

I would recognise that voice anywhere. Even in this place which is so bright I can't really see him. It is Kairi. This place is familiar. I have a memory of being without my shell. When I was swallowed by the snake on Mu, I saw Naho in this place. Then I could choose to return to my shell on Mu, but this feels different. At that time Naho approached me but I know I have to approach Kairi. He is surrounded by wisps of darkness. I realise they have form. They are Maymuans, swooping around my twin. I can see him between the spaces of their murmuration.

I step towards Kairi and one of the swirling shadows reaches out to me. A scream catches in my throat. The palm reaching out for mine belongs to Aito. I instinctively reach out for him but the spectre of his hand slips through my fingers. I hold my hand steady until it is almost as if we are touching. My hand immersed in the shadow of his hand. Aito's face, even in shadow, is beautiful. He looks at me with longing. I wait for him to speak but no sound comes.

"He's okay. Our son Ren is well." I sob and Aito's shadow is sucked back into the swirl encircling Kairi.

Another hand reaches out to me. This one I can hold tight. Kairi pulls me through the shadows, and I stand facing him for the first time in over ten orbits.

"They are the shadows of those I killed." Kairi explains.

I shudder at the number of victims Kairi has amassed. There must have been so much violence in his new land. I am not surprised but what does shock me is the transformation of my twin. In his voice I hear something I have never heard before. Remorse. And physically he looks perfect. Gone are the terrible scars from his violent initiations. His skin is as unblemished as when we were maymu on Mu with the rearers. I look at my own hand and my little finger, chopped off by a rearer on Mu after being stung by a scorpion, is restored.

Kairi smiles and he glances to the side. I follow his gaze and another shock awaits me. It is the unnamed who was sacrificed on Mu. I last held her torso on Mu.

Takanori victorious with her severed head. But here, she also is restored. Her dark skin glows and her hair is a familiar halo of curls.

She runs towards me and cuddles my legs. I kneel down and we hold each other tight.

"I felt your love," the unnamed says, "and his too. You are not so unalike."

I look to Kairi in surprise.

"I have to go now." The unnamed says untangling herself from my tight grasp. I don't want her to go but I know she must. I give her one final squeeze and watch as Kairi gently kisses her forehead. She skips through Kairi's shadows leaving us alone together.

I stare at him for a while with nothing but the gentle whoosh of his shadows to allay the silence. He stares back. The impatience and fury which characterised our time together on Mu, gone.

"Why are you here?" I ask eventually.

Kairi smiles, "It is my duty to greet you."

"How did you die?"

A frown creases Kairi's face for the first time in this place, "Ultimately by my own hand. I made many mistakes."

The shadows surrounding us swirl faster.

"Who greeted you?" I ask. It surely couldn't have been Takanori.

"Naho."

"Naho?" I echo in surprise, "Why didn't she wait for me?"

"She doesn't need to greet you. It can be anyone who loved you."

I take a deep breath and exhale. What remains of my shell is flooded with confusing emotions.

"What are you saying? That you love me? You had a horrible way of showing it."

Kairi does not flinch from my gaze, "I love you. I always have. When we were maymu our love was so pure, but I got lost."

"Takanori." I whisper.

"Yes Takanori. He groomed me to do exactly what he wanted and then I couldn't stop. Even when I was free of him in my new land, I wasn't strong enough to return to love."

"You make it sound so simple, but it was horrific to live through." I say, unwilling to let Kairi so easily summarise the hell we all endured.

"I have had a long time to think about it, with these for company," Kairi says ruefully, gesturing to his shadows, "Do you know about the prophesy?"

"Yes," I say, "Remember when we were in the snake hunt cave? And you forced me to get you a snake?" I can't resist adding. Kairi doesn't rise to the bait instead he just nods, and I continue, "You told me there was a ankh above an opening. It was true! I went back and it led to a secret chamber underneath the Experienced temple."

"What?" Kairi gasps.

"Yes! There were all these crazy glyphs about us."

"Us?"

"Stop interrupting me and I will tell you."

A flicker of the less serene Kairi returns but he does keep quiet.

"They showed us torn apart. Then the volcano, the tsunami and finally Mu drowned."

"There were others you know?" Kairi says.

"Other what?"

"Twins."

What are you talking about?" I snap.

"We are not the first twins. There were other twins born on Mu. They used to kill them because they were scared of their power. They must have been terrified of that prophesy. But when Takanori became chief Experienced he started saving the water twin and only killing the fire twin."

"He never understood the power of water."

"That is what Ayana said."

"Who is Ayana?" I ask curious.

"It doesn't matter. She is the one who told me all this.

But what doesn't make sense is why I was allowed to live."

"You mean we?" I growl.

"Okay, we." Kairi concedes.

"I know a bit about this part," I say, "It seems Takanori was obsessed with making the prophesy a reality. The prophesy wasn't about all those other twins. It was about twins created in a specific way."

The shadows move closer together and the light dims in this place.

Kairi looks a little queasy, "What do you mean?"

I swallow the bile constricting my throat, "There was a glyph," I hesitate and take a deep breath, "It showed that if an Experienced violently created with a carrier then powerful twins with the capacity to destroy the island would be born. That is what he did. To Naho."

Kairi's jaw drops, "That is wicked."

"There was so much wickedness," I shout, thoughts of Naho stirring my rage, "What you did was wicked. All this he and she stuff. Splitting us in that way."

"I know." Kairi says, "I didn't know any better."

"And that makes it okay?" I growl.

"Not okay but that is nevertheless the reality."

Kairi is not arguing with me, but I still feel angry, "Did you carry all that on in your new land?"

"Yes. And I paid the price for it."

We are silent for a moment.

"What about you?" Kairi asks.

"We did for a while but there is hope. My son, who was infatuated with the idea of you by the way, chose to renounce the split." I smile thinking of the courage of Ren, "So there is hope of a new way of life."

"You are a shaper." Kairi says.

"A what?"

"A shaper," Kairi laughs, "When Naho greeted me here she told me that both her and I had been victims of the universe in our time but there are those who have the power to be shapers. You have faced down fate and become a shaper Kaori."

The light returns and I breathe. Yes, I have transformed my fate and in my time I was victorious.

"It is time for me to go." Kairi says.

"What will happen to me now?'

"You have to step out of my shadows into your own."

I look at the forms of all those Kairi killed in his time. There could only be one waiting for me. How cruel that it is he who I must wait with.

"Did you kill him?" Kairi asks.

"Yes." I say.

A hunger crosses Kairi's face. If he lingers, he may catch a glimpse of Takanori's shadow waiting for me. I watch Kairi carefully. He sighs and his faces relaxes.

"I don't need him anymore, but I can't leave this place until my love is reciprocated."

My twin waits for my mercy. I gaze upon his beautiful black skin and in the gloss of his dark eyes I see my son. Vulnerable. Hopeful. Pure.

"I love you Kairi."

We embrace and I feel our splintered hearts heal.

I step out of Kairi's shadows but find none waiting for me. I think of the confrontation in the Experienced chamber on Mu all those orbits ago. I did not strike Takanori. My snakes rushed to my defence. My hearts bursts with gratitude that I can wait alone. Not to greet Eri or Ren. They have many orbits to share together.

I sit and wait for my love, Saki.

Epilogue

KENTARO

May - Orbit Sixteen

Kentaro watches the black smoke billowing from the roof of the temple. A leaders' meeting is underway in the chamber below. For six orbits, Kentaro has waited for the right moment to strike. When the smoke thins, he will approach and scale the temple stairs. The dulling of the fire should ensure the only soul who remains in the chamber will be Ayana. Her name rattles his skinny frame. Skin clings tightly to his bones. His face is gaunt and his cheeks are hollow. Orbits spent lingering around May have rendered Kentaro unrecognisable. For the past few moons he has returned to gather information and not one Mayan recognised him as Kairi's love.

His shell is emaciated but a fire worthy of Kairi burns

in Kentaro's eyes. He stares at the roof of the temple and shudders. This is the closest he has been to the temple since that dreadful rise.

Kairi told him to run and hide. The foundations trembled with the zealousness of the Mayans tearing through the temple in pursuit of Kairi.

"What do they want?" Kentaro had asked.

Kairi did not respond but Ayana shook her head sadly and said, "They believe only the blood of Kairi will return the rain."

"That is ridiculous," Kentaro said. "Tell them! Tell them there are no gods."

Ayana drew the mayus closer to her.

"You can't let this happen. I won't let this happen."

"Go, Kentaro," Kairi said wearily.

Kentaro's head swivelled from Kairi to Ayana. Their necks were slack with defeat.

"I won't leave you," Kentaro said, the pounding of frantic feet approaching their chamber audible behind them.

"Ken-kun, please," Kairi pleaded, and it was the plea which broke Kentaro's heart and spirit.

"Come," Ayana said, herding the mayus. Riku and

Haru seemed to understand. They embraced Kairi, but Hana, panic on her face, refused to leave.

"What about Kairi?" she said.

"I will join you soon, Hana, don't worry," Kairi said.

Hana's chin trembled. "I don't believe you."

"I want to stay with Kairi and Kentaro," Kai said, trying to escape Ayana's grasp.

The collective breath of the intruders could be heard through the locked chamber door. Kairi pushed Ayana and the mayus towards the other door, through which they could escape the manic Mayans.

Kairi kissed Kai and said, "Riku, carry Hana."

Riku threw Hana over his shoulder and ran out of the chamber, followed by Haru. Ayana gave one last look over her shoulder and sprinted out, dragging Kai.

"I will not leave you," Kentaro said.

Kairi looked at the locked chamber door. It was throbbing with the furious thumps of the Mayans trying to burst through.

"Ken-kun, I love you. I always will. Please. You must ensure Kai survives."

Kairi dragged Kentaro to the door through which Ayana had just fled. "Go!"

"I love you."

"I know. Now get Kai."

Kentaro reached out and touched every part of Kairi's face, then ran after Ayana.

When Kentaro emerged, squinting into the sunlight, he saw Ayana and Haru arguing furiously about the best direction to flee. Seizing his opportunity, Kentaro snatched Kai from Ayana's grasp.

"No!" Ayana screamed and grabbed Kai's other arm. They pulled him in opposite directions until he screamed out in pain.

"Let go!" Ayana hissed.

"Kairi told me to take Kai. It will be better if we split up, then at least one of us will survive."

Ayana gripped even tighter on to Kai's wrist. "You are not taking my mayu."

A loud voice shouted, "Ayana!"

A large and a small Mayan appeared from around the corner of the pyramid.

"It's Miki and Kai's friend Kao. Leave him with us, Kentaro. She will help us. You go. Quick!"

Kentaro looked at Kai. His expression, although still afraid, had softened on seeing his friend. He let go of Kai's arm. "Please be careful, Ayana."

Ayana pulled Kai towards her and Kentaro recoiled from the venom in her face.

"What are you doing?" Miki screamed. "Don't let him go!"

Kentaro's insides turned to water. Panic surged and he sprinted towards the forest. The last he heard was Miki berating Ayana.

"Why did you let him go?"

"Because he had Kai!" Ayana roared. "Go after him before he gets too far."

Kentaro escaped, not by outrunning Miki but by outclimbing her. He scaled an enormous kaka tree and lay, trembling with the shock of the betrayal, within its leafy branches. He watched her pass many times, searching for him. It felt like he had only just begun to acclimatise to the shock when he noticed activity on the top of the pyramid. He had participated in extinguishing enough souls to know they were preparing for a sacrifice. How could his shell, or even his mind, withstand sitting here, perched in a tree, watching Kairi's execution? Blood rushed to Kentaro's head and he felt grateful to be able to pass out. But he didn't. Energy crackled through his veins and merciful darkness did not come.

Kentaro watched a swarm of she leaders assemble on the roof. Above, heavy, dark clouds gathered and Kentaro thought surely now was not the time for the rain to return? Glittering amongst the she leaders was Ayana in her ceremonial robe. A hatred that could curdle an ocean swept over Kentaro. He searched for the mayus but they were nowhere to be seen.

The mob of Mayans at the bottom of the temple

surged forwards and Kentaro stopped breathing when he saw his love, painted blue, ascending the stairs. His shell seemed oddly rigid. Kentaro prayed that someone had been merciful enough to slip Kairi a kaka draught so he would not feel anything. But who would care enough and have the knowledge of the rurals to do that?

Kairi lay on the sacrificial table. Ayana unfurled the execution tools and a fear so terrifying struck Kentaro that he almost plummeted from the tree. A memory. Of Ayana suggesting a sacrificial ritual so barbaric that he and Kairi had shuddered. Ayana had shrugged and said, "It would only be used for the most valuable sacrifices anyway."

When Ayana penetrated Kairi's neck and the rain fell, Kentaro felt grateful. What he had feared had not come to pass. He curled up and watched the black clouds open. The precious water drenched the kaka leaves, each drop on a leaf chiming a beautiful melody. Every rise Kentaro had prayed for the rain to return, but the song ringing through the branches could not soothe Kentaro's agony. Kairi was gone. He closed his eyes and willed his soul to leave his shell. To depart like a butterfly from a cocoon.

At the return of the rain, the Mayans had roared. A second even louder roar from the Mayans stirred Kentaro from his torment. He didn't want to see what was exciting the Mayans now.

He should have lain there. He shouldn't have looked back at the temple, but he did. And Ayana was blue. She was wearing Kairi's skin.

Kentaro swallows the vomit threatening to erupt from his throat. He must focus. His probing of the Mayans has confirmed what he has observed; the temple is preparing a grand ceremony to declare Kai the leader of May.

Kentaro fingers the weapons in his pockets. Kai will never be leader. Ayana and all of her mayus will be slaughtered before the moon has a chance to settle in the sky.

The billowing smoke has become a whisper in the dusk.

Kentaro crawls up the outer staircase, careful not to disturb any loose rocks. He glances at his palms. They are blue from the dust of the sacrificed staining the steps. Although too many orbits have passed, Kentaro hopes he is carrying a fragment of Kairi with him. He wishes he had Kairi's power to engorge the ebbing flame of the fire pit and incinerate all within, but he is a rural and can only use the land.

Kentaro moves towards the open hatch leading into the meeting chamber but is distracted by the sacrificial table. He paces around it, stroking his fingertips against the stone warmed by the setting sun. He stares into the space where Kairi's beautiful head would have lain. A sob catches in Kentaro's throat. What would Kairi say? *Real May don't cry.* He kisses the stone and returns to his duty. *Destroy Ayana.*

The room appears empty. Kentaro leans further over the hatch and sees her. She is alone. He scurries back and prepares the weapons in his pockets. Wrapped tightly in leaves are several darts dipped in a deadly undiluted kaka draught. Kentaro loads three into a thick hollow gamgam-type stick. He inhales and rolls into position over the hatch and exhales, shooting three darts directly into Ayana.

Her hand brushes away the darts as if swatting a fly, but when they clatter to the ground she looks at them and then looks up, and with horror sees Kentaro leering down. Ayana manages one step before she collapses and slumps to the floor, unheard words gurgling in her mouth. Kentaro leaps into the chamber, sprinting down the stairs and advances over her. With a kick he rolls her over and she glares up at him.

"I never trusted you," Kentaro spits. "I knew you were a snake but I thought…" Kentaro sighs heavily and looks around the chamber, his eyes stopping at the raised platform where he, Ayana, and Kairi would sit and reign over the others.

"He loved you. Do you know that? You filled the hole

left by Kaori. But you were more to him than a twin. He loved you as he loved me. He desired you. I thought you loved him!" Kentaro yells, "How could you do this?"

Ayana holds Kentaro's gaze.

"Look! Even now you are not sorry. Well, you will be because I am going to kill you."

Ayana blinks. Kentaro leans over so he can read every emotion in her eyes. "And I am going to kill Riku, Haru, Hana, and Kai."

Fear flashes in Ayana's eyes but Kentaro can also sense doubt.

"You don't believe I am capable of such depravity, do you?"

Ayana's eyelids narrow.

"I saw what you did to Kairi's shell.'

Finally Kentaro sees what he desires in Ayana: terror.

"I will never *ever* forget the sight of you wearing Kairi's skin. You are a despicable, wicked she and as long as there is breath in my shell I will hunt and destroy your mayus."

Although Ayana cannot move, panic radiates from her shell, but there is nothing she can do.

"Listen," Kentaro says, over the sound of bare feet slapping on stone. "Someone is coming. Perfect. One of your mayus will die now."

Tears stream from Ayana's eyes.

Kentaro loads three more darts. "I am sure you

tormented Kairi in his final moments with your wicked words."

Kentaro raises the blow dart to his mouth and Ayana's eyes widen in shock. "I have had enough of you in this time. Your mayus will join you soon."

Kentaro blows three darts into Ayana's face. Her pride, fear, and fury disappear. Ayana is no more. Kentaro checks her neck to ensure blood no longer pumps around her shell. He plucks the darts from her face and gathers up the ones from the floor.

Kentaro folds them back into the leaf and returns them to his pocket. He faces the opening and Reo walks into the chamber.

Kentaro stumbles backwards. *What is Reo doing here? He disappeared on Mu. How the ratty hell can he be here on May?*

"Ken-kun?"

It is not Reo.

"Kai?" Kentaro asks, searching for the mayu he remembers in the face of this fully grown Mayan.

"I'm so glad you are here!" Kai says and scoops Kentaro up in an enthusiastic hug. "You are so skinny. Where have you been?"

Kentaro struggles to catch his breath and Kai continues, his voice lowering, "You know what happened to Kairi after you fled. I am not judging you," Kai says quickly. "It was a wild time. Kairi, he was so incredible. He volunteered to be sacrificed! Can you believe it? My Ayana did it. Then the rain came back. It was amazing. Where is she? Have you seen her? Does she know you're back?"

Kai peers at Kentaro with a purity that weakens Kentaro's resolve. Kentaro licks his dry lips and swallows. A shadow falls over Kai's face.

"Are you okay Ken-kun? What's going on?"

Kentaro involuntarily glances at Ayana on the floor and Kai notices her for the first time.

"Oh no!" Kai drops down to Ayana and gasps when his fingers feel the chill of death on her face. "She's dead."

"I know," Kentaro mumbles.

"What happened? Did you see anyone?" Kai looks wildly around the chamber, searching for assassins, unaware the threat is before him. He sobs and rests his head on Ayana's lifeless torso, oblivious to the three dart pricks on her face which would alert him to his fate.

Kentaro withdraws a leaf of fresh darts from his pocket and rocks backwards and forwards on his heels, trying to build momentum to complete his vow of vengeance. He is not the mayu, Kai, Kentaro tells himself. He is not the mayu who fought to sit on your knee; who loved to watch you weave. The last of the fire pit crackles and hisses as its end draws near.

"No!" A loud voice shouts from across the chamber.

Miki and Kao run towards Kentaro. He panics and drops the wrapper of darts. Kao reaches him first but runs straight past him to join Kai at Ayana's side. Miki picks up the wrapper, stares at Kentaro, and says,

"Thank you for returning. How did you know Ayana was ill?"

Miki hands Kentaro the wrapper of darts and he is incapable of releasing words from his mouth.

"Ill?" Kao asks.

"Yes," Miki nods. "Ayana has been … unwell for a while."

Miki does not take her eyes off Kentaro. He stares back at her. Why is she pretending Ayana died naturally? Miki switches her gaze to the wrapper in Kentaro's hand. It is as if she can see through the leaves straight to Kentaro's deadly intent for the mayus.

"Kai," Miki barks, "show Kentaro the fire."

Kai looks at her as if she has sprouted another head. "Why?"

"Show him now," Miki demands.

Kai and Kao exchange a puzzled look, but Kai reluctantly gets to his feet, glares at Miki, then stares into the fire. The dying embers rattle and a magnificent flame erupts from the pit.

Kentaro almost drops the wrapper again. He stares up at the fire licking the roof and sees Kairi's face scorched into ceiling.

"Your turn, Kao," Miki says with a grim smile. Kao is already standing. She expected this strange request. She pushes her mane of curls from her face and Kentaro gasps. He looks from Ayana's lifeless face to Kao's face, which glows in the light of Kai's flame. They are the same.

Kao's shell is curled in a little; she bites her lip and her eyes flicker from Kentaro to the floor.

"Ignore him," Miki snaps. "How you forgotten all that Ayana taught you?"

Kao blushes and Miki continues berating her. "You can't harness the power with hesitation. You are about to rearrange the stars. Stand up straight and be proud of what you can do."

Kao nods and straightens her spine. She inhales and Kentaro feels a force tug him forwards. Above the hatch, thunder rumbles. A bolt of lightning strikes Kai's flame and rain pours into the chamber.

Kai, forgetting the horror of the moment, fights Kao's rain with a stronger flame. They smile at each other but then they remember: Ayana is dead. The flame recedes and the raincloud soars from the hatch.

Kentaro staggers into a puddle created by Kao. He shoves his weapons into his pocket and holds his head in his hands. The magnitude of what he has just witnessed is too much to bear.

"Leave us," Miki instructs Kai and Kao.

Kai looks at Ayana and reaches for Kao's hand. "No. You can't tell us what to do, Miki. We are not going to leave Ayana. Or Ken-kun."

Miki approaches Ayana and kneels down beside her. She gently strokes her palm down Ayana's face, closing her eyelids. Carefully, Miki rolls Ayana until she is on her side and looks as though she is sleeping.

"Let her rest now," Miki whispers.

Kai and Kao look uncertain as to what to do.

"Leave us," Kentaro says. "Please. I must speak to Miki alone."

Kao tugs at Kai's arm but Kai will not allow her to lead him out. He shakes her off and seizes Kentaro by the shoulders. "Promise me. Promise me you won't leave again."

Kentaro squirms in Kai's tight grip.

"I need you. Please don't leave me," Kai pleads.

"I won't," Kentaro mumbles and Kai finally lets Kao drag him from the chamber.

"Thank you," Miki says.

"Thank you?" Kentaro scoffs. "What the ratty hell is going on? What did I just see?"

"You saw magnificent twins alive on May."

"It is impossible," Kentaro says, though the quiver in his voice suggests otherwise. A dark thought clouds his face. "Are they Kairi's? Did Kairi and Ayana create on Mu?"

Kentaro barely breathes while waiting for Miki's reply.

"No," Miki says, putting him out of his misery. "They were created by Ayana and Reo. Let me explain."

Kentaro is desperate to interrupt but he lets Miki continue.

"Kaori and Kairi were not the first twins born on Mu. There was a prophesy. The prophesy of the three hearts which predicted the birth of doomed twins – the carrier twin cursed with the power to control water and the other cursed with the power to manipulate fire. The prophesy terrified the Experienced. It has terrified them since it was first discovered many, many orbits ago. Long before you and I. All twins born on Mu were executed."

Kentaro shivers. "Except for Kairi and Kaori? Why?"

"I don't know. Perhaps Naho knew, but what I do know is when Takanori became the chief Experienced he secretly saved the water twins. Kaori and Kairi were the only fire and water pair saved but there are many solo water twins. Hana is a water twin."

Kentaro's eyebrows shoot up in surprise.

"Ayana was also a water twin. So you know what that means, don't you? She lost not only her own twin, but also the fire twin she birthed and who was slaughtered. You cannot imagine what she has suffered."

"You cannot imagine what I have suffered!" Kentaro roars and Miki takes a step back. "I saw her! *Wearing*

Kairi. Can you imagine what it did to me to see that? The shell I have loved all my life peeled like a ratty ganba fruit. How do you think I feel?"

Miki sighs. Her hand twitches as she considers trying to physically console Kentaro, but she knows he would not want her touch.

"I always said the May was too strong in Ayana. Many terrible events have occurred both here and on Mu. And you have all suffered greatly."

Kentaro's anger refuses to subside. "But this still doesn't make sense. When Ayana arrived on May she could barely walk her belly was so heavy. She had Kai on our side of the island. I was there! I saw her!"

"What did you see?" Miki asks.

"I saw Kai being born!" Kentaro shouts in frustration. "Ayana was hanging from Kairi's neck. She was squatting. It was wild. Then he came. Kai. He slid onto the floor."

"And then?"

Kentaro hesitates. "Then she asked us, Kairi and me, to bathe him immediately. She said it was important for him to be cleansed in salt water."

"And when you left, I was waiting. Ayana delivered another and I took her."

"But how did you know the first would be a he?" Kentaro snaps, desperate to believe he has not been deceived.

"We didn't. Ayana knew she was carrying twins. She could feel them. We agreed that you and Kairi could never know. Whoever came first was destined to live with you on May side of Mu and the second was taken to Sana."

"Sana?" Kentaro splutters. "Root leader Sana? What does she have to do with any of this?"

"She agreed to raise Kao in secret and love her like her own. When the time was right, she joined you all on May. With her mayu, Kao."

Kentaro squeezes the bridge of his nose between his eyes. Vivid memories threaten to burst through his forehead.

Kai never without his shadow Kao. Outside the temple, in the temple. Always together. Sana's audacity to declare herself the leader of her tribe after Matsu's death. Sana! The first she leader on May.

"You shes are unbelievable!" Kentaro spits. "How dare you plot all this! Right in front of our faces!"

Miki does not flinch. After all she has seen, Kentaro's anger barely raises her heartbeat.

"You are as devious as sea snakes."

"Perhaps." Miki shrugs. "But there are important things we must discuss. There are powerful twins alive on May. The twins Kao and Kai. What will you do, Kentaro?"

Kentaro puts his head in his hands and claws at his face. "Do they know they are twins?"

"No," Miki says.

Kentaro lowers his hands and they stare into each other. For the first time, Miki looks unstable. It is as startling as witnessing a mountain tremble.

"Don't kill them," she pleads.

The chamber is still.

"Kairi wouldn't want you to."

"Don't tell me what Kairi would want, you ratty devil!" Kentaro yells.

Miki inhales Kentaro's fury but does not give up. "Do not kill them. You can tell them they are twins. You can guide them. Don't you see? Twins Kaori and Kairi can live! This time without hiding their powers."

At the mention of Kairi's name again, Kentaro attempts to speak, but Miki refuses to be silenced.

"I could have killed you just now instead of pretending Ayana died naturally," Miki says simply.

Kentaro's eyes narrow and he dips his hand into his pocket.

"Don't bother," Miki says wearily. "I didn't kill you because in you I see a future. You have a pure heart, Kentaro. Many experiences have tarnished it, but a pure heart beats in your chest. To follow Kairi, you concealed your mu. He extinguished his but yours is simply dormant. You can guide these twins. You know you can. In balance and harmony. With may and with mu."

Kentaro takes a trembling breath. "I could but…"

"But?" Miki sighs in resignation. "I cannot live."

"That's right."

"I know." Miki frowns. "But you cannot scare them. They will believe you returned because Ayana was dying, but if they find me dead at your feet too, they will know."

Kentaro nods, his whole shell trembling.

"What is on your darts? The root of the kaka tree?"

Kentaro nods again.

"Inject me with one. I can walk out of here but you know my heart will stop before I reach the shore." Miki draws up her sleeve and offers Kentaro her vein. He feels like he should apologise, say something, but the words don't come. He thinks of her betrayal after leaving Kairi alone in the temple. He slides a dart out of the wrapper and pricks her forearm.

"I am sorry for your suffering." Miki looks from Ayana's shell on the chamber floor and back to Kentaro. "You can choose what happens next. What this land is to become. Do you want to keep putting your hand in the fire to honour Kairi? Scoop up embers which will only scorch your palm? Or will you choose to transform as only fire can, with water at your side, guiding you along paths that seem impenetrable?"

Miki gently places her hand over Kentaro's heart. He accepts her touch. "Lead with love."

Miki turns and walks from the chamber. Her footsteps fade and are replaced by the slap of eager feet.

Kao and Kai sprint through the opening and Kentaro sees them as innocent girnums in flight, no longer with the faces of Ayana and Reo. Instead, he sees Kaori and Kairi, soaring into the chamber, scaling trees for honeycomb, sharing roasted coco.

Kentaro wipes the tears from his eyes and opens his arms wide.

Kai and Kao swoop towards him, ready to settle in a new nest.

Weaving the World of Mu

The Mu Chronicles documents the fate of forbidden twins Kairi and Kaori. A major theme across the trilogy is how the twins are split. Two halves of an imperfect whole. The twins have been psychologically torn apart by the Maymuan society which demands conformity and perfection. On the ancient island of Mu, it is a cultural norm that all people have may and mu. In present society we would describe this as masculine and feminine traits.

Takanori, the zealous leader of the Experienced, declared the twins incomplete. It was decided Kairi was pure may. Fire and extreme masculinity. Kaori was pure mu. Water and extreme femininity. The twins, in their own ways, spend their lives trying to restore balance within themselves, heal their psychological wounds and become whole again.

I am interested in the idea of being incomplete or 'half' because of my own life experiences. I was born in Liverpool, England in the 1980's. At that time, I was referred to as a half caste child because my parents are both mixed race Black British and my maternal grandmother was white British. Half caste is now correctly considered an offensive term. Having the 'half' identity bestowed upon me at birth from the society I grew up in was extremely damaging. I never felt whole. I felt a longing for a coherent identity. A longing which remains with me to this day.

I experienced devastating racism growing up on a council estate in Knowsley. This type of discrimination still plagues Knowsley as evidenced by the riots outside of a Knowsley hotel, housing asylum seekers in 2023.[1] As a child, white adults would use racial slurs as I passed their homes. In school, racist words would be scrawled in textbooks depicting any Black and Brown people and conflict with other pupils would always result in them calling me racist names.

These are examples of white people attacking the Black 'half' of my identity, but this also occurred the other way around. Black people would attack my white 'half'.

My maternal aunties are white British. When I would

visit my cousin in London the local Black kids would say he could not be my cousin because he was white. And if he was my cousin then I must be a coconut. Brown on the outside and white inside. This description has haunted me. I didn't grow up in a Black community. Knowsley in 2011 was 97.2% white in the 1980's the percentage would have been even higher (In 2020 it had changed to 95.3% white). [2] The Black community in Liverpool is the oldest in Europe[3] mostly centred around Toxteth in the south of the city. According to the 2001 census 38% of the population in Granby, Toxteth were from ethnic groups other than white British.[4] Some of my paternal relatives still live in Toxteth but my parents moved out to Knowsley before I was born.

Since publishing Book One of the Mu Chronicles, I have been invited to several glamourous publishing events. One such event was the inaugural Black Writers Guild[5] conference in London in 2022. It was a delight to be surrounded by phenomenal Black writers who seemed at ease in their own skin and fully aware of their power. At lunch I mentioned to another writer that I had never tried jollof rice. He laughed but then realising I was serious said, 'Really'?

I wasn't raised on jollof rice despite my West African heritage. I wasn't raised on rice and peas either despite having a Jamaican great uncle. My ancestry is from Guyana and Sierra Leone, but I am a third-generation immigrant. At home we had boil in the bag white rice with sweet and sour sauce cooked from frozen. It was something easy for my working parents to prepare. As well as chicken kievs, crispy pancakes and corned beef hash. I enjoyed it but this is white working-class food, and I am not white. These working-class meals are never on the menu in publishing parties no matter the colour of the participants' skin. I spent a decade living in Japan where I had the illegitimate privilege of being perceived as a brown European. A status higher than an African American, South Korean or a Chinese person living in Japan. I can make various Japanese dishes, but I can't make a single dish from Guyana or Sierra Leone. Even in something as simple as food I don't feel Black enough.

The other area in which I am 'split' is sexuality. I am bisexual and it has taken forty years on this planet to be able to describe myself in this way. At a time when a wonderful plethora of nuanced terms to define sexuality have entered the mainstream. There are now words which more accurately describe my sexuality, but I felt so ashamed for so long about being bisexual that it is important for me to really own that word.

When I was younger, I wished that I was either straight or gay so I could feel whole but I'm not. I am bisexual. A close friend once told me there is no such thing as a bisexual which really hurt because I had accepted his sexuality entirely and the same was not reciprocated. I have faced constant accusations that I am not really gay. In my late teens I had a girlfriend, and I came out to my parents. It was a terrible experience, and she never met my family. They have never met any of my female partners.

I was married to my ex-husband for 14 years and our marriage erased my bisexuality. I had no queer identity. I could pass through the world as heterosexual with all its privileges. My life before my marriage dismissed as a phase or an experiment. It seems as if society says a bisexual woman is only bisexual when her current partner is a woman. It was challenging because at times I felt like I was closeted but on the other hand it felt futile to assert I am bisexual when I was in a monogamous heterosexual marriage. Since my marriage ended, I have come out. Again. This time I was not seeking permission it was a statement of fact. Publishing Beneath the Burning Wave with a bisexual protagonist helped me reach a place where the opinion of others no longer influenced who I choose to love.

I would like to linger on this word. Love. It is so simple, but it has been the only way through all of the confusion, shame and pain I have experienced in my life about my various identities. In the Mu Chronicles it is love that ultimately heals the twins and it is in love that they both find peace.

I am aware that talking about an abstract like love may seem trite when Black and Brown people in the UK face systemic institutional racism, live in a country who's soil is soaked with the blood of an empire and colonialism. Even in my own industry, publishing, year after the year the statistics reveal limited opportunities for Black people to progress. Homophobia is still rampant in the UK and the relentless attacks on transgender people by the mainstream media have made day to day life dangerous for trans people and anyone who is gender nonconforming.

I have certainly experienced despair and hopelessness, but I realised that looking outside of myself will not provide answers. I have a certain level of privilege which enables me to close my front door and be safe. The turmoil is within, and I have had to learn to love myself and accept myself as I am and try not to be destroyed by the burden of double consciousness[6].

It has been a long journey to self-acceptance, and it is a road I will travel for the rest of my life. I will never be Black enough or gay enough in the opinions of some people. Neither will I ever be white or heterosexual. So, what is left? Love. Love for those who try and stuff others in neatly labelled boxes. Love for those who fear difference. But first and foremost, love and respect for myself so that at the very least when I face society, I can do so knowing exactly who I am.

To truly love it is important that we all understand what we mean when we talk about love. It is not naïve, or weak. Love is the most transformative power in the universe. In her beautiful book All About Love bell hooks says, 'Imagine how much easier it would be for us to learn to love if we began with a shared definition. The word "love" is most often defined as a noun, yet all the more astute theorists of love acknowledge that we would love better if we used it as a verb.'[7]

We would most certainly love better if we used love as a verb. Love is an action, a state of being.

And in my experience love is freedom.

Jennifer Hayashi Danns

June 2023

[1] https://www.bbc.co.uk/news/uk-england-merseyside-64611823

[2] https://www.ons.gov.uk/visualisations/censusareachanges/E08000011/

[3] https://www.liverpoolmuseums.org.uk/liverpool-black-community-trail

[4] https://en.wikipedia.org/wiki/Demography_of_Liverpool#cite_note-14

[5] https://www.theblackwritersguild.com/

[6] 'It is a peculiar sensation, this double-consciousness, this sense of always looking at one's self through the eyes of others, of measuring one's soul by the tape of a world that looks on in amused contempt and pity.'
W.E.B Du Bois, The Souls of Black Folk. (New York, Avenel, NJ: Gramercy Books; 1994)

[7] bell hooks, All about Love: New Visions, (New York: HarperCollins, 1999) p.4.

Glossary

Mu he / she
Mir his / her
Mem him / her
Mers his / hers
Memself himself / herself

Ankh symbol of life

Bahm profanity
Barmuna peacock-type bird
Benme tree palm tree
Bugir string instrument
Buha toucan-type bird

Carrier pregnant person

Cobs corn
Coco coconut
Creating procreation
Creation hut mountain hut for procreation

Experienced island elder

Gamgam bamboo
Ganba citrus fruit
Gebun medicinal plant
Genmo honey bird
Ghili chilli pepper
Girnum songbird
Glyphs words, written and spoken
Gobu cotton
Gubaga scavenger bird
Guma leaf medicinal plant

Habim jungle tree
Hand group of rurals
Hunmir wood fragrant wood

Kakanumbing medicinal plant

May male
Mayan pronounced [MAY–an]
Maymu child up to age five years old

Maymuan island person
Maymuans island people
Mayu Mayan baby
Megg plant hemp-type plant
Mignu berry poison berry
Mimin sunflower-type flower
Momu Momu cherry blossom like plant
Morgon lily-type flower
Mu island name
Mu female
Mymig profanity

Nabgar vulture-type bird
Namu devotion to
Namu Experienced devotion to the Experienced
Namu May Mu devotion to the island of Mu and its people
Nimi root contraceptive
Nullos seagull-type bird
Nunum drum

Obi belt
Orbit one year

Pack group of hunters
Preparer island person with food preparation role

Ratty profanity
Rearer island person with childcare role
Rise morning or day

Taka means honourable; also hawk

Unnamed islander under twelve years old

Acknowledgments

Thank you to my mentor, Daisaku Ikeda. Nam Myoho Renge Kyo. And to all the SGI UK members who have supported me in faith.

Thank you to my original editor, Bethan Morgan. You have been the most wonderful introduction to publishing.

Thank you to the fabulous Jennie Rothwell and Ajebowale Roberts for their additional editorial support. Thank you to the entire One More Chapter Team, lead magnificently by Charlotte Ledger, for all their sincere work on this book. Thank you to Odera Igbokwe for another incredible artwork and for bringing the story so vividly to life. Thank you to the One More Chapter design team for another gorgeous cover.

Thank you to Arts Council England for a project grant which bought me time to write this book.

Thank you to my wonderful agent Ed Wilson for all of his invaluable advice.

Thank you to my children, Midori and Airi, I love you both so much. And Princess Chloe.

Thank you to Katie for all of her love and encouragement. Thank you to Millie for inspiring me with her original stories and extraordinary creativity and thank you to Jack for also inspiring me with his vivid imagination and creativity.

Thank you to Anna Mavrakakis for her love and sincere joy for my publishing dream coming true.

And finally, thank you, my readers, for crossing the scorched sea where our journey together ends. For now…

The author and One More Chapter would like to thank everyone who contributed to the publication of this story...

Analytics
Emma Harvey
Maria Osa

Audio
Fionnuala Barrett
Ciara Briggs

Contracts
Georgina Hoffman
Florence Shepherd

Design
Lucy Bennett
Fiona Greenway
Holly Macdonald
Liane Payne
Dean Russell

Digital Sales
Laura Daley
Michael Davies
Georgina Ugen

Editorial
Sharmilla Beezmohun
Arsalan Isa
Charlotte Ledger
Lydia Mason
Ajebowale Roberts
Jennie Rothwell
Kimberley Young

Marketing & Publicity
Chloe Cummings
Emma Petfield

Operations
Melissa Okusanya
Hannah Stamp

Production
Emily Chan
Denis Manson
Francesca Tuzzeo

Rights
Lana Beckwith
Rachel McCarron
Agnes Rigou
Hany Sheikh
Mohamed
Zoe Shine
Aisling Smyth

The HarperCollins Distribution Team

The HarperCollins Finance & Royalties Team

The HarperCollins Legal Team

The HarperCollins Technology Team

Trade Marketing
Ben Hurd

UK Sales
Yazmeen Akhtar
Laura Carpenter
Isabel Coburn
Jay Cochrane
Alice Gomer
Gemma Rayner
Erin White
Harriet Williams
Leah Woods

And every other essential link in the chain from delivery drivers to booksellers to librarians and beyond!